THE UNCERTAIN JOY

The Uncertain Joy

by

Patricia Robins

Dales Large Print Books
Long Preston, North Yorkshire,
BD23 4ND, England.

British Library Cataloguing in Publication Data.

Robins, Patricia
      The uncertain joy.

      A catalogue record of this book is
      available from the British Library

      ISBN   1-84262-310-9 pbk

First published in Great Britain by Hurst & Blackett 1966

Cover illustration © Heidi Spindler by arrangement with
P.W.A. International Ltd.

The moral right of the author has been asserted

Published in Large Print 2004 by arrangement with
Claire Lorrimer

Dales Large Print is an imprint of Library Magna Books Ltd.

Printed and bound in Great Britain by
T.J. (International) Ltd., Cornwall, PL28 8RW

To Mr Watts, teacher of the deaf,
in grateful appreciation

ONE

It was nearly six o'clock when Dick Allenton let himself into the flat. He was tired and on edge after an exhausting day. The Labour Government's plan to nationalise steel had caused a lot of extra work for the stockbroking firm in which he was a junior partner. Moreover, Dick, himself, had invested a considerable amount of money in shares and it was beginning to look as if the gamble he had taken when he bought them was not going to pay off.

He put his briefcase down on the hall table and stood for a moment running his hand through his fair hair. Perhaps, he thought, there was a time when he would have confided his worries to Tamily but now the prospect only flitted through his mind to be instantly rejected. Tam hated town life, even though they were lucky enough to escape every weekend to their lovely farmhouse in the country. They had been saving for years to raise sufficient capital for Dick to give up stockbroking and earn his living farming. Last year, when young Richard was born, Dick's father, Lord Allenton, had offered to subsidise him but pride had prevented him

9

accepting his father's generous offer. After all, it had been his father's idea in the first place that Dick should learn to stand on his own feet financially. One day Dick would inherit the beautiful Manor House that had been in their family for generations and, with it, the two thousand acre farm adjoining his own small house and few hundred acres. As it was, his father was running Dick's farm in with his own until Dick could afford to take it over himself.

It was bad luck that the rising costs of farming had pushed Dick's goal further and further out of reach. It was still possible to make money from a large acreage such as his father owned; but much harder to earn a living if you had only a few hundred acres.

The birth of young Richard had also made it more difficult to save. They already had a daughter, Mercia, now nearly five years old. She was, in fact, Dick's niece. He and Tamily had adopted her when Dick's sister had died soon after her husband was killed in a motor accident, and they looked upon the little girl as their own.

Dick walked into the drawing-room which was also the dining-room. The carpet was littered with toys and Richard's playpen took up what little remaining space there was. Dick flopped into one of the armchairs, too tired even to get himself a drink.

But it wasn't so much physical tiredness,

he told himself, as depression. After all, he was still only in his twenties and he had no right to feel so exhausted by a moderately hard day's work. Depression and worry were responsible for his dejection. He must have been mad to risk so much of their savings on the stock market. No one could know better than he how easy it was to lose as well as to make money on such speculations. He had not told Tamily about it, hoping that he would be able to surprise her when the time came to announce he'd made a nice little profit.

'Damn it!' Dick swore softly. It could so easily have gone for him instead of against him. Now, unless things took a miraculous turn for the better, he'd be forced to tell Tamily that it might mean another year before they could give up the flat and go to live permanently at Lower Beeches.

He could hear Mercia's high-pitched voice from along the passage where she slept with the baby, Richard. Tamily must be putting them to bed. Presently, he would go along and kiss them both and tuck them in for the night. Normally he loved this task. Mercia was a tiny, dainty Dresden-doll little girl – very like his sister whom he had loved devotedly. Sometimes, seeing Mercia, he would find himself projected back into the past when he had been a child. How happy he had been in those days. Life seemed so

11

uncomplicated then. Tam was a funny, long-legged tomboyish child, the daughter of their housekeeper, Jess, and the devoted companion of his sister who was an invalid; his devoted companion, too, for Tam had loved him wholeheartedly and deeply then.

Then? Dick's eyebrows rose questioningly. For surely Tam had gone on loving him. She had remained loyal through his silly boyhood affairs and finally, when he'd come to his senses and married her she had forgiven him that shameful affair with Carol the American girl. Many young wives would have found it impossible to forgive unfaithfulness such as his; but Tam went on loving him despite everything.

Why, then, should he suddenly doubt that love? Was he only imagining it or had Tammy changed in some indefinable way?

'Be patient and undemanding, Dick,' the doctor had said after their baby was born. Tam had had a very bad time giving birth to Richard, and for weeks after she had been terribly depressed. The worst part of all, was that she had seemed to turn against him, her husband. The perfectness of their physical relationship was suddenly gone. Tammy had not wanted him near her.

'Give her time, Dick!' the doctor said. 'Give her lots and lots of love and understanding but don't expect too much from her for a little while. It'll come back if you are patient.'

He had not understood but he'd done what the doctor advised and been gentle and understanding. When Richard was three months old, Tam had agreed they should once more share a bedroom and the baby's cot should be moved into Mercia's room. But even then, she had not been willing to return to their earlier wild passionate love-making.

'If you want to, Dick!' she said, and he had been desperately hurt, knowing that she herself felt no desire for him.

Since then they had returned to a more normal married life but somehow it wasn't the same. He always felt that he was the one who needed her; that she would have been quite happy if he left her alone. Unfortunately, they never talked it out. When Dick brought up the subject, Tammy somehow managed to avoid any discussion about it. It was as if all the love she had to give was lavished now on the children; on the baby in particular.

'People who are mature are not jealous of their own children,' he told himself. But it was small consolation. He did not mind how much love and time Tammy gave the children provided she still had some left over for him. But she gave herself to him now as if it were a duty rather than a pleasure and, because of this, they made love less and less often. If she noticed at all, Tammy did not seem to mind and this hurt, too.

They never rowed or argued. Sometimes Dick wished they did. At least it would show Tammy had some emotions he could touch. As it was, he never seemed able to reach through the barrier of her quiet reasonableness; her preoccupied manner. It was almost as if she were living in a private world of her own, excluding him.

She was never like this with the children. He could hear her now singing to them, her voice young, gay, unguarded. He knew that presently she would hug them in turn, kissing their soft warm cheeks, cuddling them in her arms. Yet when she came back into this room, she would offer her cheek for his kiss and ask him politely what kind of day he had had. How long a time it seemed since she had come rushing to him, flinging himself into his arms, warm, eager, loving...

Dick got up and poured himself out a drink. As a rule he would push such thoughts out of his mind. He was not by nature given to introspection. He liked life to be gay, to be fun, to be full of excitement and, above all, to be carefree. Perhaps it was the aftermath of a thoroughly unpleasant day. No man could be carefree at the thought of a couple of thousand pounds chucked down the drain. He was probably exaggerating the problem of his relationship with Tammy.

He downed his drink and lit a cigarette, feeling better. Viewing it sensibly, he told himself, there was no problem. He loved Tammy and she loved him. They had Mercia and the baby son they both adored. All marriages had to quieten down after their honeymoon phase wore off. He was probably the unreasonable one, expecting Tammy to have the same physical desires as himself. The fact that in the earlier days of their marriage she had met him on equal terms in this respect, was no reason to suppose she had stopped loving him just because she did not want to make love any more. She was probably tired with the children to look after, the shopping and cooking to do. Not that Richard was any trouble. He was an amazingly good baby, half the trouble Mercia had been at the same age. She, too, was easy enough to manage now. Since her fourth birthday she had been going to a nursery school nearby during the week and she was far less spoilt and demanding than she had been in the past. All the same, he must not forget Tammy had been very ill after Richard's birth and the doctor had warned him it would take time for her to recover fully.

'Oh, Dick, you're home!'

Tammy came across the room and, as Dick stood up, presented her cheek. Some strange

15

impulse made him kiss her suddenly and unexpectedly on the mouth. Her lips, though soft and unrejecting, were nevertheless not responsive. There was a faint look of surprise in her brown eyes.

Dick grinned disarmingly.

'If you will come near me smelling of baby powder, soap and everything wholesome, you can't complain if your husband wants to kiss you properly.'

She did not reply and, watching her, Dick wondered suddenly if she had heard him. Then she said abruptly:

'Would you go and say good night to them? Mercia won't settle until you've been in.'

He turned away from her, trying not to feel hurt. Perhaps, he thought as he walked down the passage, he'd picked a bad moment. She would be wanting to go and put the supper on; her mind would be on domestic matters.

He went into the children's bedroom. The baby was nearly asleep. His starfish hands were spread out palms upwards above his curly fair head. The blue eyes looked dreamy. Dick felt his heart melting. The child was beautiful. Actually, he had hoped before he was born that their baby would look like Tammy. He'd been disappointed that Richard had arrived nearly an exact replica in miniature of himself! But now he no longer saw the likeness. Richard was just his son, tiny, perfect, defenceless, needing his love and his protection. In that tiny body lay the power to bring out everything that was best in Dick. He was more than just a son; he was the living proof of his and Tammy's love for one another.

'Good night, boy!' Dick said, touching the soft cheek with his hand.

'You didn't kiss him!' Mercia whispered from her bed.

Dick smiled down at the little girl.

'He's nearly asleep,' he whispered back, sitting down on the fluffy pink blanket and permitting the child to climb out of bed on to his knee.

'Have you been a good girl today?'

The blue eyes looked wide and innocent.

'And has Richard been a good boy?'

'No! He burst my balloon. He did it on purpose. He wasn't even sorry!'

Dick smiled.

'I'm sure he was. I expect he got a nasty fright when it went off "bang"!'

'He didn't!' The little rosebud mouth screwed into a pout. 'He didn't even *cry!*'

'Well, I'll buy you another balloon tomorrow. One of those long sausage balloons. How about that?'

'With a face?'

'With a face!'

He lifted her back into bed and tucked her up. She clung to him, her thin little arms

17

round his neck as she hugged him tightly.

'Do you love me best in all the world, Daddy?'

Laughing, he shook his head.

'Why not?'

'Because I love Mummy as much as I love you and because I love Richard as much as I love you, so you see, I just can't love you best.'

'But I *want* to be loved best!'

'One day someone will come along who will love you more than anything in the whole world!'

'A prince?'

'Maybe!'

'Will he love me the way you love Mummy?'

'Yes! Now go to sleep.'

'I think you should love me more than Mummy!'

'Go to sleep, Mercia. You'll wake Richard.'

'Well, it's true. I love *you* best so you ought to love *me* best!'

'Well, I love you best of all the little girls in the world. Now, *go to sleep!*'

He turned out the light and walked back down the corridor smiling. Not yet five and yet already she was a little woman, full of coquetry, playing up to him. Strange the way kids sensed things. Young as she was, she knew Tammy meant more to him than anyone else.

Tammy was in the kitchen. He paused in the open doorway and stood watching her as she stood with her back towards him decorating the pastry on a pie. He longed to go up and put his arms round her and kiss the back of her neck which looked white and thin and vulnerable beneath the dark brown hair. But something prevented him from this perfectly natural action, keeping him silent and unmoving in the doorway.

'That you, Dick?' She did not turn round. 'Put the oven on for me, will you? 400 degrees. Thanks!'

'Shall I bring you a drink?'

'Not just now – I'll have one in a minute.'

'Anything I can do?'

'No, thanks. I've laid the table. I won't be long.'

Feeling dismissed, he wandered back to the drawing-room and began to tidy up the toys. He folded away the playpen and poured himself another drink. Depression was settling down on him again.

'Thank goodness we go down to Lower Beeches tomorrow,' he thought.

He and Tammy loved the farmhouse. All their most treasured possessions remained there and this flat was furnished with odds and ends. It was merely a convenient home. At the weekends they had Sandra, a local girl, in to help with the children and the housework and the cooking and Tammy

19

could relax; have the rest she needed. He, Dick, would be able to wander round the farm with Adam Bond, the bailiff, renewing contact with the land, discussing the progress of the barley or the rise in the price of wheat. He could go into the cowsheds and stand contentedly watching the electric machines effortlessly extracting the milk and passing it down the pipes to the cooling machine and from there into bottles. A modern, efficient dairy herd of prize Guernseys.

Bond was a first-class fellow. Dick liked him and knew that Bond put far more thought into the farming of Dick's land than he need. But then Bond never forgot that he owed his life to Dick who had rushed in to save him being gored by a bull way back before Richard was born. Everyone then had thought that Bond was going blind but he'd gone off to America for a miracle operation and returned to his old job with Dick's father a new man.

Dick liked and respected Adam but he was never quite at ease with him when Tamily was around. Somehow he was unable to forget that Tammy and Adam had come pretty close to falling in love that time he'd been chasing around after Carol. Of course, Tammy had explained to him afterwards that she'd only thought twice about Adam because she was hurt – on the rebound. All the same, she never denied that she liked him very much indeed and they were still exceedingly good friends. Tammy seemed to be able to relax completely when she was in Bond's company; to talk and laugh and be quite her old self. He, Dick, had no reason to feel jealous but he was hurt that Tammy seemed to prefer Adam's company at the weekend to his own. Not that Bond ever intruded. He refused most of Tammy's invitations to stay for meals and only very occasionally spent the evening with them. But he was never very far off – or so it seemed to Dick – and Tammy was always so pleased to see him.

Once, when he mentioned it to her, she had looked at him in surprise.

'But, Dick, he is Richard's godfather and he so loves the children. Why shouldn't he come up and see them?'

It had not seemed to occur to her that Bond might have been enjoying her company, too. To be quite fair, Dick had to admit that Bond never excluded him; was as interested in Dick's conversation as Tammy's and was never over-attentive to her. He was always courteous and considerate but never unduly so. Yes, Dick could not help but like him though he would have liked him more if Tammy had liked him less.

Suddenly Dick's natural good humour reasserted itself.

'I'm making mountains out of molehills!' he chided himself. 'My finances may be in a rocky state but there's nothing wrong with my marriage. I'm more in love with Tammy than ever!'

The thought surprised him. It was true – she was seldom out of his thoughts for long nowadays. He was always looking for ways to please and surprise her. He wanted to give her things and as he couldn't afford the big ones like mink coats and jewellery, he gave her little surprises like flowers and chocolates and perfume. In the early days of their marriage it had never entered his head to make such gestures. It had been the other way round then – Tammy had been always thinking up little ways to surprise and please him. Of course, he realised she hadn't time now – not since Richard had been born. He had to accept that she was a mother as well as his wife and she managed both jobs very well. It was only as a mistress she failed him...

Dick's thoughts came to an abrupt halt. He could not understand why his subconscious should be unearthing such strange conclusions this evening. At least, he presumed they were in his subconscious for he'd certainly never thought quite this way before. But now it was out, he knew it was the way he really did feel. Tammy was just not his partner in love any more. There was a strange invisible barrier between them, a barrier which somehow he intended to break down.

'Maybe things will be better this weekend,' he told himself. It was May – a beautiful month when Spring had settled upon the countryside, fresh and green in the fields and the woods full of bluebells and ragged robin and Star of Bethlehem. He'd felt the excitement in the air last time they were down. The squirrels were out of their winter hibernation, darting up and down the beech trees, full of purpose, sometimes daring even to come on to the lawns. The sky was full of the first swallows, dipping and weaving and calling to their mates. Everywhere animals were seeking their mates, building their homes, raising their young. There were new calves with soft liquid black eyes fringed with long, long lashes, nuzzling against their mothers; all the young things newly born into the big exciting world. Yes, Spring was exciting, invigorating and beautiful. Something in Tammy must feel this, too, for she was as close to the country as he was; it was something they shared because of their shared childhood, playing together in those same fields and woods, swimming in the same streams. Tammy had always known what he felt – she must feel his need even if she felt none of her own.

'I'll have that drink now, Dick. Supper

won't be long. What sort of a day did you have?'

He leant forward impulsively, suddenly eager to discuss his day with her. But the words never came. He could not tell her about the shares – not yet. Maybe after the weekend...

'Pretty horrible!' he said, getting up to pour her a glass of sherry.

'Never mind! We'll be away from it all soon – only another three months and we'll be back at Lower Beeches for good. I can't wait for it. By the way, did I tell you there's someone interested in renting the flat? A Mrs Fletcher who's a friend of the woman upstairs. She's willing to take over the remainder of our lease provided we'll guarantee vacant possession by the end of August. I told her that we would be out a month before in all probability.'

Dick's hand, holding the sherry decanter, shook and the amber liquid dripped over on to the carpet.

'What's the matter?' Tammy asked, taking the glass from him. 'That's all right, isn't it?'

'Yes ... yes, of course, though I don't think you should give her any definite date just yet. I mean, I can't be sure of weeks, can I? I must do my bit at the office until everyone has had their summer holiday ... and my replacement–'

'Are you trying to tell me we aren't going

home in August after all?'

Tammy's voice was quiet but with an undertone which increased Dick's disquiet.

'No, of course not – it's just that I think you're being a little premature. Leave that side of it to me, will you, Tam? And as to when you go home – well, you can always go ahead with the kids if you can't stick it up here any longer, you know that.'

Tammy gave him a long, searching look. It was as if she could sense intuitively that there was something more behind his actual words. But all she said was:

'No, if you've got to stay, we'll stay with you!'

Dick stubbed out his cigarette angrily. He was feeling guilty about his shares and he hated that urge to gamble that had made him risk their savings. It was so silly. He could be careful enough of other people's money, but his own ... well, he'd been so sure it would work out all right, despite the fact that the firm's policy to their clients had been in opposition to buying.

He was going to have to tell Tammy but not tonight. She would be upset and worried and he couldn't blame her if she were fed up to the teeth with him. Somehow he couldn't bear the thought of widening the gap between them.

'Well, there are more important things to worry about than Mrs Fletcher!' Tammy said enigmatically. 'Besides, the pie will be burning. Do you want to eat here or in the kitchen?'

'I don't mind!' said Dick quietly. 'Kitchen if it's easier.'

He followed her down the passage but suddenly he had no appetite. He was hungry enough but not for food. He wanted what he was beginning to realise he had lost – Tammy's love.

He sat opposite her, looking at the thin, fragile face, the huge dark eyes and wide mouth.

Was it true, he asked himself, that he'd lost her love? If it *was* true, he could not think of any reason why.

TWO

Tamily sat in the deckchair on the lawn and closed her eyes. The sun was warm against her face and arms and she began to relax. It was always the same when they came home for the weekends – the tensions eased slowly but surely, and by Sunday afternoon she was just able to steel herself to face the ordeal of another long week in London.

She hated London; hated the small confines of their flat; hated the long winter afternoons when outside the streets and houses and even the trees looked grey and distant. In the summer, the concrete and tarmac roads and the roofs and chimneys shimmered in a harsh glaring light which seemed to hurt her eyes. Even in the park when she took the children for their afternoon walks, the dust and soot lay thick on the grass and trees, hiding their true summer green.

Tamily knew that other people saw London in a different light. To them it held excitement, adventure and was stimulating and invigorating to their senses. But she was a country girl and city life would always be alien to her. Here in the country she was at

27

peace – or as much at peace as it was possible to be with that never ceasing worry nagging always at the back of her mind.

It was Richard who was the cause of the worry; the cause of her sleepless nights and preoccupied days. It was more frightening because it was nameless; because she could not state reasonably and concisely exactly what was wrong. But she could never rid herself of the feeling that something was wrong.

At first she had kept such thoughts to herself. Until she could pinpoint her feelings, she could not bring herself to impart her fears to Dick. But one day, a few months ago, she had blurted out:

'Do you think there's anything wrong with Richard?'

Dick had looked astonished.

'Wrong? In what way? Do you mean ill?'

Already she was wishing she had said nothing. Haltingly she tried to explain.

Dick laughed. Not unkindly but simply in negation.

'But of course not, Tam. Why, I never saw such a fat, healthy-looking child; intelligent, too. Look at the way he tries to talk … gurgling away twenty to the dozen. And he's as good as walking. I never saw a child brighter or more chirpy in my life!'

Everything he said was true. Richard was a big strong baby, yet not too fat. His cheeks were a lovely healthy red and he ate and slept well and was very little trouble to manage. He watched everything that went on around him and copied what he saw.

All the same, there was Something...

It crossed Tamily's mind that, feeling as she did, she could put her mind at rest by taking him to the doctor for a complete check-up; or to the child welfare clinic. But although she even reached the point of having him dressed and ready in his pram, in the end she never went. It was as if such positive action might lead to the confirmation of her fears. They might be given a name.

'Yes, Mrs Allenton, you're right, he isn't quite normal... He's a very mild spastic case, Mrs Allenton...'

Even in the warm sunlight, Tamily shivered. How stupid she was being. Dick saw nothing wrong; Jess, her mother, and Dick's parents, all thought Richard was quite perfect. She was the only one and she couldn't put into words what she felt. Any sensible mother would have gone to the doctor, had her baby checked over fully and been able to go home with her mind at rest. Why shouldn't she be like the others?

Tamily sighed. It was the same old argument that went on inside her day and night remorselessly. No wonder she was thin and pale looking! Jess would be up to tea with them presently and she would be sure to say, just as she had every weekend: 'You should

29

eat more, Tamily, you're far too thin!' Her
mother and Lord and Lady Allenton all
believed that it was London which was
dragging her down. Only Adam guessed
there was more to it than that.

'Everything all right between you and
Dick?' he'd asked this morning when they
were alone for a moment in the kitchen
having a cup of coffee before Adam went off
with Dick.

'Yes! Yes, of course!'

'But something's on your mind, isn't it?
You know I'd do anything I could to help if
you felt like confiding.'

'Thank you, Adam, but I'm all right, really.'

Maybe she would tell him. The friendship
between herself and this tall, strong man was
something very special. Once, before Richard
was born, she had wondered if she was in
love with Adam but that was only because
she'd been so desperately disappointed in
Dick. She'd forgiven Dick his unfaithfulness
and put Adam out of her mind, knowing that
she had exaggerated her affection and pity for
him into something more than it was. Now,
of course, there was no need for pity. Adam's
sight had been fully restored and there was
no danger of a recurrence of his blindness.
The affection remained.

Tamily wondered if Adam was still in love
with her. There was little doubt that he had
loved her although he'd only once spoken of

his love but it showed in a
ways when she had needed l
he did still care he never inc
way except by his extreme
towards her; his obvious p
company and his strange in
innermost thoughts.

In a way, Adam was closer to her than
Dick. He was more sensitive to her feelings;
more deep-thinking and intuitive than Dick.
But that wasn't Dick's fault. He tried so hard
to understand and be patient with her. His
nature was to skate on the surface of life,
taking the fun and the gaiety and sunshine
that life had to offer and avoiding the pitfalls
of depression and unpleasantness. His was a
happy, sunny disposition, uncomplicated
and perhaps, unmeaningly, a little selfish. It
was this very insouciance in his temperament that had always attracted her to him.
It wasn't fair of her to complain about it
now, at this stage of their marriage when he
had never tried harder to consider her and
make her happy. She knew that Dick had
never loved her more than he did now and
yet the gulf between them seemed to be
widening rather than decreasing.

It was, she realised, her fault. Dick had
been very patient with her. She had been
very ill and depressed after Richard's birth
and perhaps not entirely responsible for her
actions. Something strange had happened to

had turned against poor Dick, to see him or have him near her. Of , the doctors had explained to her that view of what had happened before Richard's arrival, during the latter half of her pregnancy, a feeling of antagonism towards Dick could have remained in her subconscious, only to show itself later, after the reconciliation, when she was ill and barely conscious of what she said and did. It would wear off as she got stronger, they said.

She could not fully understand what had happened. She had, after all, forgiven Dick for being unfaithful to her. They had made up their estrangement and become lovers again and she had pushed all memories of the Carol affair into the back of her mind. Life had seemed easy and wonderfully happy again. Then in the weeks of only semi-consciousness that followed Richard's arrival, she had seen Dick as someone to be feared, haunting her in strange and horrible nightmares, taunting her, threatening her, hurting her. These same nightmares were peopled with others, too – her mother, a shadowy background figure trying but unable to save her from Dick; and Adam. It was Adam whom she would strive to reach in her dreams; Adam who, with arms outstretched towards her, promised safety, a haven, a refuge; Adam who alone could rescue her from this insanity.

32

Gradually the nightmares had ceased and her thoughts had become more rational. Dick came to visit her and sat long patient hours by her bed, holding her hand and telling her how worried and unhappy and lonely he had been without her. It had seemed so silly that she could ever have been frightened of him! He was touchingly thrilled with the baby, hiding his disappointment that their son did not look like her but like him. He'd got over that, of course, and he really was a wonderful father to Richard, spending hours playing with him, talking to him...

Tamily's thoughts came to an abrupt halt. Yes, Dick would talk to Richard and, watching them together, Tamily could see Richard really listening, trying to imitate 'Dad-Dad-Dad'. Yet when she herself sat near the playpen singing nursery rhymes to him as once she had to Mercia, he paid no attention, sometimes not even bothering to turn round from his play. He seemed only responsive to Dick and very occasionally to Mercia when the little girl climbed into the playpen with him, to play Ring-a-Roses, shouting and laughing and bouncing Richard up and down. He loved to be picked up, rocked and cuddled and tickled, gurgling and laughing and clutching at her with his hot little hands, sometimes burying his face against her neck like an affectionate puppy.

Nothing was wrong, nothing, and yet...

33

'Mummy, Mummy, here's Jess!'

Mercia's shrill little voice carried across the lawn to Tamily. She looked up and saw her mother coming towards her, holding Mercia's hand. Richard, building bricks in his playpen, continued playing with his usual placidity.

'Hullo, dear, I do believe you're thinner than ever. I'm sure you aren't eating enough...'

Tamily smiled as Jess lowered herself into the chair beside her. Jess, too, was thin and always had been.

'I saw Granny and Grandpa fast asleep!' Mercia said. 'And do you know, Grandpa hadn't any teeth. Jess says old people have false teeth. Have you got false teeth, Mummy?'

Presently the child went off to pick bluebells and Tamily was left alone with her mother.

'I expect you are counting the days till you come down for good,' Jess said. 'Not long now.'

'No, and Dick says we could come anyway and he'll join us for weekends.'

'Why don't you do that?' Jess nodded. 'It's a very sensible suggestion. The children prefer the freedom of the country and the clean air is so much better for them.'

'All the same, I think we'll stay with Dick, until he can come, too.' Tamily's voice was unusually sharp. Jess gave her daughter a sideways glance.

'Tamily, I know this isn't any of my business, but you aren't taking that line because you don't trust Dick?'

Tamily shrugged her shoulders.

'I don't know what made me quite so vehement, Mother, but I suppose mistrust is at the back of it. After all, how can I have complete faith in him after what happened? Maybe that was partly my fault for leaving him alone all week in town – if I'd been up there with him, it couldn't have happened.'

'My dear, if you are going to forgive someone, you have to make yourself forget, too. You can't go on reminding yourself of the past and it isn't as if Dick has ever given you cause to doubt him since, has he?'

'No! But anyway, whether I've forgotten as well as forgiven is beside the point. Dick wouldn't want me to leave him... I'm sure of that.'

Something in Tamily's tone caused Jess to look at her searchingly.

'Nothing wrong between you two, is there?'

'No, why should you think so?'

Jess let it pass. Secretly, she was worried about her daughter. Tamily was never a noisy child but nor was she moody. Since little Richard was born, she had become very withdrawn, remote and silent. There was no laughter in her face; no real joy in her voice. It was as if something inside her had died. Had Tamily lost the baby, this strange behaviour would have been understandable. As it was she could find absolutely no cause for Tamily's depression. Dick was loving and attentive – far more so, Jess thought, than he had ever been in the past when he'd really led Tamily rather a dance. Dick was like that; he'd hurt people's feelings without knowing he'd done so. There was never any deliberate harm in him but he'd been spoilt as a boy and only now, as a man, had he learned to put other people before himself. Jess could see no reason to fault Dick's behaviour, so there had to be another cause.

She reminded herself that her daughter had been very dangerously ill after Richard's birth. For a time they had lived in fear that she would never fully recover. But mercifully, those months were well behind them now and Tamily had gone to live in London with Dick and the children, apparently completely well again. This recession did not make sense and Tamily either did not want to talk about herself or else even she did not know what was wrong.

Jess bent down and scooped Richard out of his playpen.

'He *is* a good baby!' she said proudly. This was her first and only grandchild, for Mercia was not related to her, dear as she was to

Jess, who loved all children. 'Lady Allenton was showing me some old photographs of Dick at this age – they are almost identical. Of course, when we first knew Dick he was about ten, wasn't he?'

'Eight!' Tamily said, her face relaxing into a smile. 'I suppose he was spoilt – we all spoilt him, didn't we?'

'You more than anyone!' Jess agreed smiling. 'You were his shadow, remember? I used to worry about you – afraid you'd be hurt when he went off to boarding school and perhaps dropped you when he came home again. But he never did.'

'I was almost as much a boy as he!' Tamily said. 'Bowling to him, racing him swimming, beating him up the highest tree. Actually, I had enough tact always to let him beat me.'

'It never crossed my mind that one day you two children would get married. When you think about it, Tamily, it is rather like a fairy tale. After all, I was only the housekeeper and you – well, I know that nowadays no one holds it against illegitimate children but the fact remained you had no father and Dick was Lord Allenton's heir. They've been wonderful to us, haven't they?'

Tamily nodded. No one appreciated her in-laws more than she. Dick's parents had loved her throughout her childhood and had welcomed her into their direct family line when Dick said he wished to marry her.

As a wedding present they had given them Lower Beeches and the farm which Dick would soon be managing. They had been very very fortunate.

Suddenly her depression vanished. Richard was sitting contentedly on Jess's lap staring sleepily at the branches of the beech tree waving above him. He looked utterly normal; a perfectly happy, healthy toddler. How silly she was to worry about nothing.

'I'll go and get tea!' she said. 'Sandra put it ready in the kitchen after lunch so I've nothing to prepare. You stay here with the children.'

She put the kettle on to boil and sat on the edge of the kitchen table to wait. Adam and Dick would be in presently. She would make the big brown pot – Dick always said tea never tasted as good in anything else. She lifted the damp white napkins covering the plates of sandwiches Sandra had left ready. Tomato and egg, cheese and cucumber, Dick's favourite. She smiled suddenly, remembering Dick as a little boy coming home from prep school for exeats saying: 'Good-oh! Cuko sandwiches, my favourite!' She and Mercia, Dick's sister, would sit watching him eat steadily through the plateful, forgoing their share so that he could enjoy the lot. How long ago those days seemed and yet the sight of the thin green slices of cucumber could take her back in an instant to their childhood.

The thought suddenly crossed her mind that maybe she and Dick were at a disadvantage having known each other so long. There were no new discoveries to make about one another. She knew all his virtues, all his faults. In a way, she understood him better even than she understood herself. It didn't help to be too aware of someone else's feelings – not when that someone was your husband. It was impossible to ignore the fact that Dick was hurt by her refusal to make love as often as he wished. She tried hard not to let him know she did not want him. Sometimes she succeeded and Dick went to sleep happy and content. But there were other nights when he would get up, hurt and humiliated, and sleep the rest of the night in the spare room. They never discussed the matter. Dick wanted to, she knew, but she felt she could not talk about it. That part of her emotional make-up was something she did not understand herself so she felt there could be no point in trying to make Dick understand what had happened to her. It was equally incomprehensible to her that a woman who had once loved her husband as passionately and warmly as she had loved Dick, could, without warning or reason, as suddenly cease to need him in that way. She didn't want any man. Richard's birth seemed to have destroyed all desire in her.

Once, and only once, she had spoken of it to her doctor. He had tried to explain that as her health and strength improved, so would her natural desire for Dick return. But that was months ago and now she would go out of her way to avoid physical contact of any kind, however slight, in case it led them to something more.

When Dick took her hand in his and held it as sometimes he did when they were sitting watching television in the evenings, she could no longer concentrate on the programme but would sit, tense, anxious, uncomfortable, seeking an excuse which would enable her to withdraw her hand from Dick's without hurting his feelings by making the gesture obvious. Yet she did not mind when Adam touched her. Sometimes he would take her hand when they were walking through the woods together. He would do so as naturally as he took little Mercia's and usually at the same time as he grasped the child's. It seemed simply to be right and natural and the feeling she had was of affection without commitment. There was never any fear or tenseness when she was with Adam...

'Tea ready?' Dick's voice behind her made her jump.

'Calm down, darling, it's only me!' He came up behind her and rested a hand lightly on her shoulder. She felt the muscles jump and her body tensed. Dick bent his head and touched her hair with his lips.

'Smells even sweeter than the hay!' he said, his voice husky.

'The kettle's boiling!' Tamily replied, jumping down from the table with a feeling of relief. 'Could you carry the tray, Dick?'

She filled the teapot and went ahead of him. He stood watching her, his eyes puzzled, a slight frown on his forehead. Had she really no idea how lovely she had looked, sitting on the table with a wide beam of sunlight slanting across her head and shoulders, warming the soft whiteness of her skin so that he longed to touch it? Of course, she had had to move but if only it could have been to take the kettle off the Aga and turn back to him, opening her arms to him...

'Hell, I'm being stupid!' Dick told himself sharply. 'We're four years married, not newly-weds. I'm expecting far too much of her. I'm at fault, not Tamily.'

He followed her on to the lawn and sat down on the grass, first lifting Richard off Jess's lap and taking the child on to his own. Mercia, ever feminine, came running to join them.

'I want to go on your lap, Daddy. It's my turn now. Put Richard down. I want to get on your lap.'

'Come and sit on mine instead!' Adam said, laughing as he joined them, catching the little girl round the waist and tossing her

41

high in the air while she squealed with excitement and delight.

Tamily and Jess watched them. Dick medium build, lithe, fair, wiry rather than tough; Adam tall, broadshouldered and strong but with gentle hazel eyes which had been so miraculously restored to sight. He was quite a lot older than Dick and Tamily and yet age did not seem important in this strange, quiet man. His quietness was part of his success with children and animals; he could soothe with a touch or a word. His whole personality was soothing, Tamily mused, whilst Dick's was of a controlled energy which could be tiring simply by its existence. He was like a tightly coiled spring which one could not help but expect to explode in one direction or another. With Dick, children were apt to become over-excited even while they were attracted to this element that found an echo in their own wild energies. They loved his company but frequently ended in tears.

Richard, of course, was too young to be affected yet. He was a placid, quiet child for the most part, although recently Tamily had noticed sudden swift, violent rages which seemed to her to be inexplicable. Perhaps only imagined.

'I must watch myself!' Tamily thought as she turned to her mother and in an ordinary casual voice, asked, 'Would you like another cup of tea?'

THREE

'Tammy?'

In the darkness, his voice sounded uneven, uncertain. She felt his hand on her arm and her muscles stiffened.

'Tammy, darling, what's wrong? Something's wrong, isn't it?'

'No, of course not. Why should you think so?' She was half whispering and yet there was no need. The children's room was at the far end of the landing and Sandra slept in the room beyond. There was no one to hear them. Nevertheless, Dick's voice was little above a breath in the darkness.

'You're always so quiet! As if you aren't quite in the same world as the rest of us. You'd tell me if something were worrying you, wouldn't you?'

'Yes!'

'Good!' He accepted the lie she had told so easily. Why had she lied! Why hadn't she said: 'Yes, I'm worried. I'm nearly going out of my mind worrying about Richard but I don't know what I'm worrying about!'?

She felt him move closer to her and she said quickly, defensively:

'I'm just tired, that's all. I expect a good

night's sleep will make me better tomorrow.'

She sensed his hesitation and held her breath waiting.

Dick let her go. It was no good – she did not want him. Maybe her excuse was perfectly genuine and she was tired. She certainly looked it. London obviously did not suit her and the sooner she came home to live, the better...

Dick shivered. She wasn't coming home so soon after all. Because of *his* mistake. It would mean a long hot summer in London which would make Tam even more exhausted. He must persuade her to come down with the children and leave him there on his own. But how? There had been a time when they'd lived apart during the week and he joined her here at weekends; but it had been a difficult unhappy time of the marriage and they had both vowed they'd never lead separate lives again, whatever the reasons which might make it advisable.

'Whatever we do from now on, we're going to do together!' He could remember the moment he had said those words; the night she had come out of hospital and they had really been reconciled. How marvellously happy they had been that night. It seemed that their love for each other had grown even greater with the recent danger of separation foremost in their minds. It horrified him to realise how nearly he had lost her; Tammy, his girl, his sweetheart, his wife. They had discovered their intense pleasure and joy in each other to a degree they had never reached before.

Yet where was that need for one another now? How could it have disappeared so completely? He had not changed. He needed her as much as ever ... but Tammy, she was different, *different*. He could have understood it if she'd been unable to forgive his infidelity. But she had forgiven him completely and they had been perfectly reconciled. If he could only know the reason...

He held his breath for a moment listening to Tammy's breathing beside him. Was she asleep? Instinct told him no. Yet he was convinced she wished him to believe she was.

Quite suddenly Dick was hit by the thought that there could be a reason his wife no longer wanted him – she *wanted someone else*. That would explain everything. But who?

For the second time in his life, Dick felt the sickening pangs of jealousy. It had to be Adam. There were no other unattached men in their circle of friends. Adam's fondness for Tamily was almost a family joke. Many a time they had teased her about her 'faithful slave'! Tammy just smiled. He had never objected, knowing how devoted Adam was to the whole family; to the children in particular.

Dick had been completely certain of Tammy's love for him. He had put out of his mind the day he had accused Tammy of being unfaithful to him with Adam, knowing in his heart that she was innocent and that he had used his accusation more as a defence for his own behaviour than from any real belief that she and Adam had overstepped the bounds of friendship. Tammy had loved him, Dick, since they were children and continued to love him with all his faults; even forgiving him ultimately for his defection with Carol. Until now, he was utterly certain of the depth and enduring quality of her love. Until now...

Dick was no longer able to lie quietly in the big double bed. He got up, put on his dressing-gown and tip-toed out of the room. If Tamily were awake and heard him, she made no sound. He went down to the kitchen and stood at the window, looking out over the moonlit garden. Somewhere among the beech trees, a nightingale was singing with violent beauty. Dick turned away, miserably conscious of the pure romantic quality of the night in contrast to his own unhappy heart.

Almost against his will, he found himself picturing Adam as he had been that same afternoon, half turned towards Tammy, his face quiet and attentive as he listened to some comment she was making. No sign of flirtation there, but then, Adam's way with women might differ from his, Dick's. Adam was the strong, silent type; a type just as intriguing to some women according to the books he'd read. Tammy herself was quiet; she had never been witty, coquettish, challenging a man openly. Yet he knew only too well how evocative her quiet deep passion could be, how rewarding. She and Adam might be two of a kind and thereby able to reach a perfect understanding.

Dick paced the floor uneasily. The more he thought about these recent months, the more suspicious and doubtful he became. There was Tamily's urgent desire to leave London for good and come down to Lower Beeches. He'd always assumed the reason was her love for the country – she had never been a town girl. But now he saw that she might be so desperate to return because Adam was here.

'I'll get my father to sack him!' he thought furiously. But he knew Lord Allenton would never comply with such a wish – not unless Dick produced positive proof that Bond was trying to entice Tamily from him and his father wouldn't easily be convinced. He had the very highest regard for Adam both as a man and as a bailiff. Adam had complete control of the whole estate and Lord Allenton trusted him as he would his own son. Maybe even more than he trusted his son, Dick thought savagely.

Although Dick was devoted to his father and knew that Lord Allenton returned that devotion, they had not always seen eye to eye. In Dick's undergraduate days, Lord Allenton had very much disapproved of him and had insisted that as future heir to the Allenton title and estate, Dick must prove himself capable of earning his own living before he gave him any part in his inheritance. Proudly, Dick had gone into the stockbroking business and had held down the job ever since, trying to save the capital needed to farm Lower Beeches independently of his father. It was partly because of the monotony of a routine office job that Dick had been led off the rails by Carol, the rich American girl who had tried so hard to get him to leave Tamily and marry her.

Dick's normal habit was to forget as quickly as possible any action of his of which he was ashamed. He had not thought of Carol in ages but now he was forced to remember because it was at that time Tammy had been lonely and become so friendly with Bond. Was it possible that Tammy had only agreed to a reconciliation because she was carrying his, Dick's, child, and a divorce at such a time would have been unthinkable? He searched his memory and the thought of those wonderful weeks before Richard's birth. Surely Tammy could not have *pretended* during that time? Nothing would convince him she had not been every bit as much in love with him as he was with her. Whatever had happened had occurred since Richard's arrival. But what?

Filled with uneasiness, Dick went back to bed. Now Tamily was really asleep and he could not bring himself to wake her as he would have liked; to talk the whole thing out with her; to ask her outright if she was in love with Bond.

He tried to put such thoughts out of his mind but he could neither do so nor fall asleep with his usual facility. Tomorrow was Sunday and in the evening they would have to drive back to London. He must get his relationship with Tamily sorted out before then. It was here in the country that they were closest. The flat seemed somehow to depersonalise them.

It was not in Dick's nature to analyse either his own or other people's emotions. This soul searching was foreign to him and, for that reason, made him nervy and irritable and on edge. He thought bitterly that it was Tammy's fault he was so depressed and uncomfortable. If she would only revert to being her usual self, he could continue his uncomplicated existence, worried only by his financial affairs – as if they were not quite enough on their own to occupy his mind.

When he woke next morning, he was

unable to rid himself of his resentment. Tamily was quiet and untalkative and he made no effort to joke with her. At breakfast he was moody and he nearly lost his temper with Mercia who tipped her boiled egg over the clean tablecloth.

'It's high time that child learned some decent manners,' he shouted, knowing he was being unfair and that it was a pure accident rather than an excess of high spirits which was responsible.

Tamily said nothing. He would have preferred her to flare up in defence of the child so that at least he could rouse some emotion in her. But although her cheeks coloured, she remained silent, going herself to the kitchen for a wet cloth to wipe up the mess.

'I didn't mean to do it!' Mercia said sulkily, looking at Dick through long silky eyelashes in a way which usually enchanted him but this morning only increased his irritation.

'You should be more careful!' he said, frowning.

Mercia burst into tears. She was a child with quick easy emotions, rather like himself; certainly not introverted. At the moment, she was resenting what she felt instinctively to be an injustice.

'You're horrid!' she shouted at him in her thin, piping treble. 'I don't like you any more. I wish you weren't my Daddy. I want

50

Adam for my Daddy.'

Dick jumped to his feet, his handsome face a mask of fury. He did not stop to consider Mercia's words at their true value or he would have known she meant nothing more than to get her own back on him. Coming as they did on top of his sleepless night, his suspicions flared into the open. Tamily, standing in the doorway, caught the full force of his fury.

'Trust a child to let the cat out of the bag!' he flung at her. 'It's you who put such thoughts into her head. You ought to be ashamed of yourself. You aren't fit to be a mother. What's more, I'm not going to stand for it any longer. You can ring up Bond and tell him he isn't welcome in this house for lunch today nor at any time. Do you hear me?'

Tamily stared at him aghast. It was beyond her to understand why Mercia's silly remark could have produced such a childish reaction. He must know the child adored him, Dick, and that Adam took only a very secondary place in her affections. To want to end their friendship with Adam on this score was too childishly ridiculous. But she would not argue with him in front of the children and Sandra, who sat staring from one to the other as if she could not believe her ears.

Dick was further infuriated by Tamily's

51

silence. She was treating him as if he were one of the children in a tantrum, ignoring him. Well, she wasn't going to go on ignoring him and the sooner she found that out the better.

'If you won't ring him, I'll do it myself!'

Tamily, busy now wiping up the spilt egg, made no sign that she had heard him. Mercia was sobbing into her table napkin, frightened by the anger she had provoked in her father. Only Richard remained impassive, spooning milky cereal into his mouth and round his face.

'Run upstairs and tidy your bedroom, Mercia!' Tamily said. 'I'll come up in a moment and see if you've done it properly. Sandra, perhaps you'd take Richard into the kitchen and give him a wash. There's as much cereal in his hair as in his tummy!'

'Well, are you going to phone or am I?'

Tamily avoided looking directly at him. She sensed that Dick wanted a row and, unavoidably, she found herself remembering last night; wondering if this morning was the result of last night's frustration. She should not have pretended to be asleep. She should have let him–

'Will you answer me, Tamily!'

'No, I won't phone, Dick. I can't think of any reason I could possibly give Adam that would make sense. If you don't want him to lunch you must make your own excuses!'

52

The quiet logic of her reply goaded him further.

'I suppose you think I don't know what is going on between you two. You think you can cover up what you really feel about each other under this cloak of being "very good friends". Good friends, indeed! He'd better keep away from you, Tamily, or there's going to be trouble. I'm warning you – warning you both. I certainly don't intend to be made a fool of by my wife.'

Tamily gasped. Dick's accusations were so unexpected that it was a moment or two before she could force herself to realise that he meant what he had said, that he really did suspect her and Adam of something more than friendship.

'But this is ridiculous, Dick!' she cried, stung at last to take up the cudgels. 'You know very well there's nothing between Adam and me. I'm very fond of him and I'm quite prepared to admit it. But as to ... well, it's so absurd I'm just not willing to defend myself against anything so silly.'

'If it's so silly, how else can you explain your behaviour of late? Do you think I don't know how you go out of your way to avoid me? Oh, I know we live together but how close are we these days? Answer me that. You may have been in love with me once but not now and don't bother to try to make me believe otherwise. You've changed, Tamily, and something has changed you. If it isn't that you are in love with Bond, then tell me what it is. Just tell me!'

Tamily sat down weakly in Mercia's chair. Dick might be wrong about Adam but he was near the truth when he said she had changed towards *him*. But he wanted a reason and she couldn't give him one. She didn't even know herself what was wrong; why she could not feel anything very deeply about him any more.

Dick watched her face, pale but with her uneasiness showing clearly in the little lines across her forehead and round her mouth.

'So you can't think of an excuse. It doesn't surprise me. Whatever faults you may have you've never been able to lie, have you, Tammy? So why not admit that it's Bond? That you're only staying with me because of the children.'

'That's not true!' She broke off, unable to say any more; unable to say what was true. 'Please let's stop this, Dick. I swear I'm not in love with Adam. I'm not in love with anyone. I know something has gone wrong between us and I'm as worried about it as you are, but making senseless accusations about me and Adam isn't going to help us. Please, Dick, don't let's quarrel when we don't even know what we're quarrelling about.'

'I know! I know that my wife is no longer in

54

love with me; no longer cares what I think or feel or do. I'm wrong, I suppose, to complain about that? You can't even understand yourself, you say, and yet you ask me to understand you. Well, I don't and, what's more, I don't intend to let things go on like this. I've been very patient with you, but my patience is exhausted. If there's something physically wrong with you, then go and see a specialist. If it's mental, then find a trick cyclist. And if it's Bond, then the sooner you tell him it's all off, the better for everyone.'

He gave her a long look, half angry, half despairing, and walked off, leaving her alone. Tamily felt her legs trembling. She could not remember when Dick had last lost his temper with her and never, never had he spoken to her in such a way. She was aghast and yet, somehow, not surprised. She could see all too clearly how he had been bottling all this up inside him and that the explosion had had to come sooner or later. Dick's was far too extroverted a nature to contain suspicion or harbour resentment. But that he should suspect Adam and herself ... even if he did not mean it deep down inside ... shattered her more even than his remarks about her health.

'It's so absolutely ridiculous!' she whispered. But quite suddenly, she knew that it was not. She did feel something more than just a casual friendship for Adam. There was a strange unspoken link that joined them; with him she could be herself and know that he wanted nothing more of her. She, in return, liked him as he was and would not have changed any part of his character had she been able to. In many ways, they were similar types, only he was male, she the female. Adam was strength and security and protection and she drew on him for all these things. Just as now, at this moment, she would have wanted to take her problem to him to ask his advice. He might understand what was wrong between herself and Dick where she did not. He might advise her, too, about her nameless fears for Richard. Yet she had not confided in him because to do so would have seemed disloyal to Dick – the one who should share her burdens. Now Dick repaid that loyalty by accusing her of being in love with Adam.

She had not heard the phone bell ring as it did when one took off the receiver to make a call. So it would seem Dick had not rung Adam about lunch. Should she let him turn up and face an atmosphere he couldn't possibly understand and was certainly not responsible for? Or should she go down and tell him vaguely that Dick and she had had a slight tiff and that Dick was in a bad mood? Adam would guess there was more behind such excuses but he would be far too tactful to question her. Maybe this was best.

She could walk Richard in his pushchair, leaving Sandra to take Mercia to church with her grandparents.

Her mind made up, Tamily hurried through her morning tasks. Dick had gone out. Probably riding, she thought. He kept his own hunter in his father's stables and usually rode every weekend. Maybe he would be calmer when he returned.

By half past ten, she was on her way to Adam's house – the little lodge at the beginning of the drive to the Manor House. Sandra's mother cooked and cleaned for him during the week but left him a cold lunch on Sundays if he wasn't invited by Dick and Tamily to join them at Lower Beeches. He had two dogs, a spaniel and a labrador, who kept him company; and, as he told Tamily, gave him something to look after other than himself. 'A dog stops one getting selfish!' he'd said. As if Adam could ever be selfish!

But before she reached the lodge, she came upon Adam in the wood that lay between their homes, his gun over his arm and his dogs scurrying in the undergrowth and barking excitedly.

'Why, hullo!' he greeted her with a warm smile. He bent and touched the baby's cheek. 'What a nice surprise! I've been out looking for an old dog fox which raided the young pheasants last night. I think Phil had the scent just now but a rabbit ran out and distracted their attention, so we might as well go home. You'll have some coffee with me? Or a drink?'

But before Tamily could reply, the dogs set up such a violent barking that Adam excused himself and dived into the undergrowth to see what was causing the commotion.

Tamily sat down by the pushchair to wait. She had enough experience to know that when a man was hunting, he would forget all else in the chase. She remembered long evenings as a child when she had accompanied Dick on one of his rabbit-shooting expeditions. No matter how cold or hot or wet, he would stride on relentlessly, determined not to go home until he had shot at least one rabbit, and she, his shadow, stayed with him. She really hated the sight of the limp, furry bodies dangling their poor dead heads out of Dick's shooting bag and yet his enthusiasm and pride infected her on his behalf, and when they arrived home she would call out just as eagerly as Dick, 'We've got two beauties!'

She smiled, remembering that childhood with its simple uncomplicated joys and companionship. She looked at Richard's fair curly head, so like his father's, and thought that it would not be long before he would be demanding his first air gun and go out with Dick or Adam to make his first kill.

Richard was becoming restless. She lifted him out of the chair and he toddled happily away on his chubby little legs, following the direction Adam had taken.

'Come back, Richard!' she called as he was about to disappear behind some trees. He paid no attention to her and she jumped to her feet, calling louder, 'No, Richard, come back to Mummy!'

Still the child toddled in, not turning his head, ignoring her. As she ran after him, she felt once more that strange uneasiness. Richard was such a good baby in every way and yet he had moments like this when he disobeyed a direct command just as if she hadn't spoken. She wasn't sure if it was stubbornness, plain disobedience or determination to have his own way at all costs. Of course, he was only eighteen months old and yet he understood perfectly well when she shook her head at him and said, 'No!' firmly that he must stop what he was doing. Then moments like this occurred when he ignored her completely...

Suddenly a shot rang out close by and fear for Richard's safety made her forget the child's disobedience. She called him again at the top of her voice and when still he did not stop, she raced forward and caught him up in her arms, half relieved that she had him safe; half angry that he had three times deliberately ignored her.

She walked back to the pushchair, carrying the boy who was showing no visible sign of annoyance because his journey had been suddenly arrested. She sat down on the grass, her legs trembling. Of course, Richard hadn't been aware that he might have wandered into a stray shot from Adam's gun, but he should have stopped when she called him so urgently. She looked into his serene, smiling face and bit her lip.

What was wrong with him? Why didn't he react as other children of his age reacted? What was the difference between him and other children of his age? She searched her memory for a picture of Mercia. Mercia had been a noisy, excitable child, frequently naughty but highly intelligent. At times she had exasperated Tamily. It was always difficult to keep Mercia in a pushchair at this age. She argued fiercely against riding in it if she wanted to walk. Although her vocabulary was limited, she was able to make herself perfectly well understood and she chattered away to herself in a mixture of real and baby words.

Tamily felt her heart miss a beat. Here lay the big difference between the two children. Richard still only made strange baby noises and even these seemed to be used less and less. Nor was he visibly affected by sounds...

Suddenly all the nameless fears of the past months crystallised into one heart-chilling thought; Richard didn't talk nor listen because he was deaf...

When Adam rejoined them, he found Tamily on her feet, her face chalk white as she stood staring down at her small son. Richard, Adam saw, was playing happily with a piece of cow parsley he was picking to pieces.

'Sorry if I startled you both. Phil was on to a fox but he was too quick for me. I had one shot and then he disappeared... Tamily, is something wrong?'

Slowly she turned her face away from the child and looked at her companion. Her dark eyes seemed enormous in her white face.

'Adam, it's Richard. When you went off just now Richard started to follow you. I tried to call him back but he just ignored me. He didn't even hear me.'

Adam put down his gun and bent on one knee beside the child.

'What happened? Was he frightened by the gunshot? He seems all right.'

She bent down beside Adam and gripped his arm through the rough tweed jacket.

'That's just it, Adam. He wasn't at all frightened. The noise didn't even stop him. I ran after him, shouting at him but he didn't even look round. Do you understand? *He didn't hear me!*'

'Now calm down, Tamily!' Adam spoke

sharply, aware of the rising hysteria in her voice. 'There's nothing to get so upset about. Maybe he didn't want to hear you. Look, I know what's worrying you but I'll prove to you there's nothing the matter with his hearing. See, I'll stand behind him where he can't see me and clap my hands.'

'No!' Tamily's voice was shrill. She clung tighter to Adam's arm. 'No, don't, *don't!*' she said.

'Now look, Tamily, this is just silly. You've got some hazy idea Richard is deaf, but you don't want me to prove he is not. Now you watch him when I clap my hands. He'll look round just like any other child would. You'll see for yourself...'

Tamily let go of his arm and clasped her hands together. Adam stepped behind the child and, before she could prevent him, he clapped his hands together. Richard continued to play.

'I'll do it again,' Adam said calmly. He clapped his hands harder but still Richard did not move. Adam swallowed, his forehead creasing into a frown, his eyes worried.

'I just don't believe it. I just *don't* believe it.'

'But you saw it. We both saw it. He's deaf, isn't he, Adam? I've known for ages something was wrong but I wouldn't let myself know the truth. There have been other things ... things that just seemed

62

strange at the time, odd, but that was all. Now I understand. He can't hear anything. He never listens when I sing to him. I think it's why he is so placid – there are no noises to distract him.'

She knelt down by the baby and put her arms round him in an instinctive gesture of protection. Adam felt his throat constrict. This, if it was true, was terrible. It couldn't be true. It just could not be true. But even as he stood there shaking his head in silent denial, the evidence of his own eyes forced him to realise that his little godson was apparently deaf.

FOUR

They argued throughout lunch and into the afternoon. Sandra and Mercia were eating at the Manor House so Dick, Adam and Tamily were alone.

'I still think we should take him to a Harley Street specialist first thing tomorrow morning,' Dick said. 'What's the point in wasting a whole day? Timms won't be able to tell you what's wrong … he'll refer you to the hospital and what can a small country hospital do compared with a Harley Street man?'

'It was the hospital who found the specialist who knew how to give me back my sight!' Adam said quietly, though for the most part he was silent, feeling that it was up to the child's parents to decide what their first move would be.

'I still want him to see Dr Timms!' Tamily said stubbornly. 'After all, he brought Richard into the world and he'll take a personal interest in him. And you know how fond of us he is, Dick. He'll know what to do.'

'He's far too old. He ought to be retiring!' Dick argued. But he, too, was fond of the old doctor. It was he who had taken young Keith Parker as a junior partner all those years ago. Keith and his beloved sister, Mercia, had fallen in love and married and Dr Timms had brought little Mercia into the world and fought so hard to save her mother's life. Dr Timms was part of their lives and yet Dick could not bring himself to trust his own son to him. Richard must have the best ear specialist there was, the best care. He must be operated on if necessary and given back his hearing. He had a horror of abnormalities and he couldn't bear the thought that his child, his only son, should be handicapped. He had such plans for him, his old prep and public school, Oxford…

'Look, Tam, let me decide what is best. I'm sure Dr Timms would agree with me. It'll only waste time for you to stay down here tomorrow. It's a damned shame you can't talk to him on the phone. Just our luck he should be away.'

'His partner said he'd be back late this evening. He has morning surgery at nine.'

'So he won't even see Richard until ten and then he's probably got to organise an appointment with the hospital ear specialist … you mightn't get anywhere at all. We must know how serious it is.'

'I'm sure you're both worrying too much,' Adam interposed soothingly. 'We know he can hear some things – for instance, he definitely listens when Dick is talking to him. Tamily's voice is so much quieter he can't hear her unless she shouts. He does have some hearing, we know that.'

'But we don't know the cause of the trouble!' Dick burst out tactlessly, so caught up in his own concern that he was not at the moment conscious of the strain on Tamily. 'Maybe he has some ear disease which is making him worse and worse. The sooner he starts some sort of treatment the better, can't you see that?'

All three looked at the baby, sleeping peacefully in his pram. He was so perfectly made it seemed unbelievable that he could have anything wrong with him. But Tamily had no doubts at all. She'd known for months and because of her stupid fears, she might have caused untold damage. If Dick were right and it was a disease, she had allowed it to go on its way unchecked all this time ... because she'd been afraid of the truth.

'We're being over-dramatic!' Adam said firmly, aware of Tamily's tension. She looked quite ill – far more in need of a doctor than Richard. 'It's probably some minor defect that a small operation can put right in a day or two – no more than that.'

'Maybe, but the sooner we know the facts the better!' Dick repeated. 'I'm all for going back to London. I know it's Sunday and we won't get anything done tonight but we can start the ball rolling first thing tomorrow morning. Leave Mercia down here with Jess so you'll be free to take Richard wherever he has to go.'

'But I don't want him handled by strangers!' Tamily protested. 'He knows Dr Timms!'

'Rubbish!' Dick said flatly. 'He's only seen him once in the last six months. If anything, he knows Phelps, our London G.P, a hell of a lot better. I've tried to see your point of view, Tam, but I can't. Any one person would back me up. You've just got some bee in your bonnet about London – you think it brings you bad luck or some such drivel. Well, I'm not going to be over-persuaded. We're going back to London with Richard. So make up your mind to it. I *know* I'm right.'

Privately, Adam agreed with him but not with his method of dealing with Tamily who was obviously suffering from shock. If only Dick could be more gentle with her; persuade her with love rather than with his rights as head of the family. He felt he ought not to be here but Tamily had insisted, even begged him to go back to the house with her; be the one to tell Dick what they had discovered; almost as if she were afraid to face Dick on her own.

'How can you trust Phelps?' Tamily said quietly. 'He's seen Richard three times in the last few months – those two injections he had to have and that time he fell out of his high chair. If he's so much more reliable

67

than Dr Timms, how come he didn't discover Richard was … was–'

'Well, how come *you* didn't?' Dick flung back at her. 'You're with him more than anyone else yet you didn't know there was anything wrong … or did you? *Did* you, Tamily?'

She couldn't face him. She simply couldn't face the look in his eyes if she told him the truth. He was so crazy about Richard. He'd never forgive her cowardice … never…

'Of course she didn't!' Adam broke in, saving her the lie that would not come. 'You know very well she'd have told you if she noticed anything strange.'

Adam, thank you, thank you!

'Well, it doesn't matter anyway. We only want Phelps to tell us the name of the best ear specialist there is, then we'll get an appointment with the specialist as private patients. If you still insist on hearing what old Timms has to say, then you can telephone him from London. He'll probably name the same man Phelps tells us to go to. Don't you agree with me, Bond?'

'I honestly don't think a day will make much difference, Dick,' he said cautiously. 'If Richard had some dreadful complaint such as meningitis he'd be ill. We don't need a doctor to tell us that he's as fit as a fiddle. I rather imagine it'll turn out to be some small deformity of the ear. In which case nobody is going to take any drastic steps tomorrow.'

Adam's calm voice at once soothed Tamily's taut nerves. But it had the opposite effect on Dick.

'What do you know about it!' he said rudely. 'We none of us know what's wrong nor will until we've seen a specialist.'

'You asked his opinion, Dick,' Tamily began, but Adam interrupted:

'Dick's quite right. It's really up to the two of you to decide this on your own. Anyway, it's time I went home… I've several things I must do this afternoon. Will you forgive me if I leave you?'

Tamily restrained the impulse to jump up and beg him not to go. Dick, mollified, said:

'Sorry if I jumped down your throat – a bit upset … you know how it is.'

He went to the gate with Adam. Tamily sat alone, her heart filled with uneasiness. How hotly she had denied that Adam meant anything special to her and yet this afternoon was positive proof of just how much he did mean. She was beginning to wish they'd never told Dick about Richard; that she'd made some excuse to remain down here on the Monday and let Adam drive her and Richard in to see Timms. Adam was always so calm and reassuring. Dick's panicky anxiety only increased her own. Poor Dick! She must not forget that

Richard was as important to him as to her.

When he came back he seemed subdued and very restless.

'I'm going up to the Manor to tell Mother and Father,' he said presently. 'Jess, too, will have to know. If you'll pack up here, Tamily, we can be on our way after tea.'

She had not the strength to renew the argument with him. She felt completely exhausted. The very last thing she wanted to do was to go back to London.

'Will you send Sandra back to give me a hand?' she called after Dick and saw him nod in agreement.

She went up to their bedroom and started to pack. As she did so, she found herself remembering their near quarrel this morning. Dick seemed to have forgotten his jealous accusations about Adam. But then, that was just like Dick. He could be right up one moment and down the next and was seldom consistent. Obviously, he didn't really believe Adam meant anything to her, although he clearly resented her attachment to Adam however innocent it might be. That, too, was typical of Dick. He needed to be the centre of attention. Being married to him was like being married to a child.

'We all spoilt him when he was a boy,' her mother had said. But surely Dick had to grow up sometime soon? He was not only a husband but a parent now and he couldn't go on being a child himself.

When he returned he was in a much happier mood.

'Father says we're not to spare expense – he'll foot all the bills if we can't afford it. Jolly decent of the old boy. He's transferring a couple of hundred pounds to my bank tomorrow morning.'

'Oh, Dick, ought we to let him? Can't we manage?'

She was unprepared for the strange look that came over Dick's face – almost as if he felt guilty about something. He changed the conversation quickly and went downstairs to pack the boot of the car.

Mercia came back with Jess and Sandra. The little girl was full of questions.

'What's wrong with Richard? Why are you going back so soon? Why aren't I going with you? Is Richard going to die!'

'Silly girl!' Jess chided her. 'What an idea!'

But Tamily felt her heart stand still. Suppose there really was something seriously wrong with Richard? Suppose it wasn't a 'minor deformity' as Adam had suggested, but a tumour, a brain tumour maybe? She couldn't bear it. Panic began to rise in her. Her mother said:

'Richard is far too bonny a baby to have much the matter with him, so don't look so downhearted, dear.'

'Yes, I'm being silly to worry when I don't

71

know how much there is to worry about.'

'You'll have to keep a firm grip on yourself, Tamily. Dick is beside himself and he'll need you to reassure him.'

'But why?' Tamily burst out. 'Why can't Dick be the one to reassure *me*? It isn't fair!'

She knew she was being childish but Jess did not reprimand her. She said simply:

'Women are usually far more stoical at times like this. Men are apt to go to pieces. You must reassure each other.'

'Mother, I don't feel brave. I'm frantic with worry.'

'Of course, but quite needlessly, I'm sure. There are thousands of deaf children and these days all kinds of things can be done to help them if an operation can't put matters right. Even at its blackest, things aren't too bad. And then there's Adam, don't forget!'

'Adam?' She felt her cheeks burning.

'Why, yes, the miraculous way his sight was restored when everyone had given up hope. Even if they tell you nothing can be done when you see the specialist tomorrow, who knows some new operation won't be perfected long before little Richard is grown up and really needs his hearing, just as the new techniques saved Adam from blindness at the eleventh hour.'

Tamily felt herself relax. Jess was right. She had no right to give way to depression.

'I'll ring you tomorrow from London,

Mother. Will you pass on any news there is to Adam? He's very concerned, too.'

'Of course, dear. Now, come down and have some tea. I know Dick's in a hurry to get away, but the children need their tea first and I've told him so.'

'If I could be firm like that with Dick, life would be a lot easier,' Tamily thought. 'But I either argue with him, or give in before he gets annoyed. I suppose I'm afraid of him, really!'

It seemed strange to her that any sane person could be afraid of Dick who never did any harm to a soul unless it were accidental. She supposed it was a legacy left over from childhood. In those days she had found Dick's disapproval unbearable. Now their roles had become oddly reversed and it was Dick who wanted *her* approval. He wanted her to love him with the old, blind, uncritical passion and she could not. Yet he was unchanged; he was the same Dick, the same boy, the same man she had married. She wondered if it was because he had hurt her so terribly by his affair with Carol that she could no longer hero-worship him. She didn't want to be vindictive and she'd forgiven Dick. If only she could forget as well as forgive! Go back to that wonderful closeness they had shared; that certainty that she belonged to him and only to him and that no matter what he did, there could never be another man she could love in quite the same way.

Tamily went down to tea with her mother. Dick had put Richard in his high chair and was feeding him small squares of buttered bread. Looking at their two identical fair heads close together, she felt her heart miss a beat. Dick could be so sweet with the children and they both adored him. Of course she still loved him.

'Dick's right to want the best specialist we can get,' she thought. 'I'm silly to cling to poor old Dr Timms just because he nursed me through Richard's birth. He couldn't do anything for Richard now. It's lucky we have the flat in Town.'

Richard looked up and gave her a beaming smile. Her heart contracting, she went over and kissed the top of his head.

'How about one for me, too?' Dick said grinning.

She hesitated only a fraction of a second before she bent and kissed Dick on the cheek. The smile left his eyes as he gave her a quick searching look. Suddenly he was gay and happy.

'Speed it up, you lot, and we'll be on our way!'

He was in a hurry now to get back to London. The first shock of hearing about Richard's deafness was wearing off and his natural optimism was returning.

Of course the boy was going to be all right,

he told himself. 'Silly to have been so worried about it. A minor op and he'll be as right as rain. Poor little Tam – looks as if she'd been hit by a bomb. I must take care of her; show her how much I love her instead of chucking silly accusations at her about Adam. As if she'd ever fall for poor old Adam! Naturally Tam *likes* him – we all *like* him but that has nothing to do with love.'

He felt the touch of her lips on his cheek and knew that it had excited him. When they got back to London he'd help her put the boy to bed and then, somehow, he'd become her lover again. It wasn't natural the way they'd been living. In his view, the doctors didn't know what they were talking about, preaching a need for time and patience. A woman liked a man to be masterful; not to plead with her to let him make love to her like some foppish weakling. He knew his Tammy a lot better than the doctors did. And he wasn't going to sit back patiently waiting any longer. With this new problem of Richard's to be tackled, it was only right that he and Tammy should get their marriage on to a firm foothold again. Secure in each other, they could face anything together.

'Ready, darling?' he asked as she put down her teacup. 'Then we'll be off!'

Jess stood watching the car as it turned through the gates into the lane. Mercia was 'helping' Sandra with the washing-up. There was no need for Jess to guard her expression and her face was lined with worry. Something was wrong apart from the distressing news about the baby. Tammy wouldn't talk about it but she knew those two children so well she was sensitive to their individual moods. Dick was edgy, as if he were controlling himself with an effort. Tam was a bundle of nerves.

Jess could not believe that Dick was playing around with another woman again. Carol had been the first and she was sure the last. Dick had nearly lost Tamily then and he wasn't likely to forget it in a hurry. Besides, Jess was sure that he loved her even more than he had when he married her. It showed just in the way he looked at her, like a young boy in love for the first time.

And Tamily! Was she, perhaps, finding it harder than she had thought, to forgive Dick? Or was she still run down? Immediately after the baby's birth, they had been in a desperate state of worry about her, but she'd slowly recovered. Jess resolved to have a word with Dr Timms ... find out if the after effects could still be lingering as long as eighteen months later.

She waited until Sandra had finished tidying up and then, taking Mercia's hand in hers, they walked slowly back along the lane to join Lord and Lady Allenton at the Manor House.

FIVE

'It isn't the same between us any more, is it, Tam?'

Dick's voice sounded hurt and bewildered. In the darkness, she reached out and touched his hand in a gesture that was half apologetic, half comforting.

'It isn't your fault, Dick. It's mine. I'm sorry!'

She knew the words were inadequate. Dick wanted a concrete reason why she had ceased to respond when he made love to her. Dick couldn't get to grips with nebulous emotions. He liked his problems fair and square where he could tackle them in the open. Poor Dick. She couldn't help him. It wasn't enough to lie there passive and unresisting in his arms. He demanded a passionate response she simply could not give him. She knew she had failed him.

'Perhaps it's just that men and women are different!' she tried again, her voice soft and pleading. 'I don't seem able to think of anything but little Richard. I'm wrong, I know, but I can't make myself different.'

'I don't see what Richard has to do with it ... with *us!*'

She couldn't explain. Dick had his emotions in separate compartments. Hers were inextricably interrelated.

'I do love you, Dick.'

'Do you?' His voice was harder, almost bitter. 'It isn't my idea of love, Tam. It used not to be yours. Sorry I forced myself on you.'

'Dick, please…'

But he turned his back on her and would not relent. For a little while, she lay sleepless and filled with uneasiness but gradually her thoughts swung back to Richard. The problem of Dick was pushed to the back of her mind. In retrospect, the day seemed to have been endless; a long nightmare from which she could only awaken tomorrow when they saw the specialist. Even then, it could be the beginning of a new nightmare. If it were a tumour…

When at last she slept, her dreams were filled with uneasiness and she awoke emotionally as well as physically exhausted.

At nine o'clock, Dick was on the telephone to Phelps. The doctor said he would see them privately, immediately after surgery. It would save time if they drove Richard round just before ten.

'You get him ready while I phone the office,' Dick said. His voice was curt and unfriendly. 'I obviously won't be able to go in today.'

Tamily cleared away the breakfast. Neither she nor Dick had eaten anything although the baby had plodded steadily through his cereal and boiled egg. At a quarter to ten, Dick had the car out and was waiting impatiently for Tamily to bring Richard downstairs. When she did not come, he went back up to the flat and found her on the telephone to Dr Timms.

'I'll just write that down,' she was saying. 'King Edward's Ear, Nose and Throat Hospital. Thank you so much, Dr Timms … yes, I'm sure he will … thank you again.'

She turned to Dick, her face flushed and eager.

'He says we should take Richard to–'

'I thought I made it clear yesterday that Phelps was going to deal with the boy.' Dick's voice was trembling with a temper he could barely control. Tamily's face whitened.

'Yes, you did. But you also said I might telephone Dr Timms from London this morning. In fact, it was your suggestion I should do so.'

Dick's temper was worsened by being put in the wrong. Moreover, Tamily's quiet, reasonable tone added to his frustration. He would welcome a good blazing row but Tamily was like a blank wall – there was nothing he could hit out against.

'For God's sake stop arguing and let's get a move on,' he said furiously. 'I can't afford

79

to waste a whole day away from the office for nothing.'

Trembling, Tamily turned and picked up the little boy. Having heard Dick's shout only as a distant muffled noise, Richard was unperturbed and as placidly content as ever when his mother carried him down to the car. They drove the short distance to Dr Phelps' surgery in a few minutes. There were still half a dozen National Health patients awaiting their turn. Dick and Tamily joined them in the waiting-room, Dick burying himself in his morning paper, already ashamed of his outburst and yet still angry because Tamily had not told him she had intended phoning Timms. He was certain she had waited until he was out of the flat so she could talk to the old doctor behind his back. It hurt to think she felt it necessary to do this and yet he was sufficiently honest to realise that his reaction would have been against her making the call at all. He intended to handle this problem of Richard his way and show Tamily once and for all that he was head of his household.

Eventually their turn came to see the doctor.

After a cursory examination, Phelps said without hesitation:

'Mr Wilmot Cosgrave is the man for you to see. He's at the King Edward's Ear, Nose and Throat Hospital. I'll see if I can get you an appointment today, though it may be difficult at such short notice. Fortunately, he happens to be my godfather, believe it or not, so he may squeeze you in.'

Dick avoided Tamily's eyes. He guessed she was thinking that Dr Timms had picked the same hospital; that there was no advantage to seeing Phelps. But he felt he would be vindicated if Phelps did manage to get an appointment for them today. After all, Timms hadn't any strings to pull with the specialist. In any event he had been proved right to come back to Town with the boy – now they were getting some action, starting the ball rolling.

Tamily wasn't thinking about Timms. While Phelps made his telephone call, she was silently praying that Mr Cosgrave would fit Richard in today. She could not stand another sleepless night without knowing exactly what was wrong with Richard.

'Well, you're lucky!' Dr Phelps said smiling. 'He will see the boy at two-thirty and he's cutting a lunch short to do so.'

Dick was triumphant. His bad humour gave way at once to cheerful optimism. He thanked the doctor warmly and bounced Richard cheerfully on his knee. His depression had gone and he felt confident that this man Cosgrave would be able to put matters right. He didn't probe too deeply into how the specialist would do this but he was fully prepared at this moment to believe that his son was not going to remain deaf for the rest of his life.

'Think I'll go into the office for a few hours,' he said to Tamily as they left the surgery. 'I'll have an early lunch and be back in time to pick you and Richard up at two. Okay?'

Tamily felt none of Dick's optimism as she tried to busy herself in the flat. Richard was having his morning nap and as there was no lunch to prepare for Dick, she hadn't enough to do to keep her mind off her worries. At least Richard hadn't got meningitis! she reminded herself wryly. The possibility of a tumour still remained. Phelps had been very vague, saying that he hadn't the apparatus with which to test Richard's hearing accurately and that they must leave the diagnosis of the cause of the deafness to the specialist.

Knowing how worried her mother and Dick's parents would be, she put through a call to the Manor and brought them up to date with their arrangements.

'I'll telephone you again tonight, Mother, when we know more about it,' she told Jess. 'And, Mother, will you pass this on to Adam? I know he'll be worrying, too.'

As she put down the telephone, Tamily felt her cheeks burning. Dick, with his stupid accusations, had made her horribly self-conscious about a friendship that until now had been completely natural and uncomplicated. Dick's absurd suggestion that she was in love with Adam had made her question her feelings and reactions. She saw Adam differently now – as Dick was seeing him – as an attractive man who might well appeal to a woman. If Adam married, which he'd denied he would, his wife would have a marvellous husband. Adam was sensitive, understanding, kind, sympathetic and yet strong and manly with it. He adored children and was wonderful with them, firm yet fair and able to come down to their level. It was difficult to find fault with him. Some people might find him dull because he was quiet and never self-assertive but it was this quietness of spirit, the lack of restlessness in his nature, which appealed to her and made his companionship so enjoyable to her.

'I won't let Dick spoil our friendship!' she thought. Dick was being childish and silly, trying to read more into it than there was. He didn't really mean it. It was just his way of hitting back at her because she had failed to give him what he wanted.

Her cheeks burned again remembering the past night. She ought not to blame Dick for failing to understand her when she didn't understand her own reactions. She did still love him but she loved him like a child. She couldn't meet the full force of his desire with equal passion. She would like to be able to lie in his arms; to be kissed and cuddled but nothing more. It wasn't easy to simulate passion. It was the more difficult because there had been a time when she and Dick had reached the very pinnacle of love and satisfaction together; when their love making had been full of fire and abandonment in one another; beautiful, exciting, perfect.

Such moments could not be pretended, Tamily thought. They could only evolve from the depth of emotional reaction. What Tamily failed to understand was that emotionally she had dissociated herself from Dick.

A few hours later she sat beside him in the hospital waiting-room, waiting to see the specialist. Dick's depression had returned. On checking his financial position at the office, it had turned out to be even worse than he had expected. His shares had fallen even further and the general view of his older, more experienced partners was that they were unlikely to climb again in the near future.

'Hang on to them, Dick – they'll come back in a year or two,' the senior partner advised him. But he couldn't wait a year or two. He wanted to go back to Lower Beeches with Tam and start farming. He'd waited long enough. Now, if the boy was ill, he'd need fresh country air. Tammy did, too, and he himself was country reared and hated flat life. If it hadn't been for weekends and holidays at Lower Beeches, he'd never have stood London for so long.

He thought about the vast sums of money he would one day inherit from his father. Lord Allenton was getting old now and Dick knew that he was ready to hand over the reins to him. It was only his pride which stood between him and everything he and Tam wanted. His father had wanted him to prove himself and Dick had sworn an oath to Tammy that he wouldn't go home until he had done so. That proving was so nearly achieved. It was the most appalling bad luck that this last gamble should have failed to work out in his favour. To go home now and admit failure to his father was more than he could bring himself to do … not even for Tammy and the children.

For the first time in his life, Dick found himself regretting the day his father had made Adam Bond his bailiff. If Adam had failed to make a success of the job, Lord Allenton might now be in a position where he needed Dick's help so badly he would be begging his son to come back. Dick could have saved his face by letting everyone believe he'd only given up his stockbroker's job to assist his father. But Adam had proved himself over and over again to be perfectly capable, not only of handling the Allenton estate and all the complicated financial paper work that went with farming today, but he ran Dick's farm, Lower Beeches, too, and with the same success. Dick's presence on his own farm was superfluous. There was no need for him to take over except his own need to be back working close to the land.

Dick hated any kind of emotional complication. He had always had a simple, easy friendship with Bond which had seemed to be cemented for ever on the day Dick had saved his life. Now, suddenly, he was torn between his liking for the man and his jealousy of him. Not only was Adam a success with his father, but with Tamily, too. He didn't really believe Tammy was falling in love with Adam – that was a crazy idea without foundation. But he was well aware of her fondness for Adam and of the curious dependence she seemed to have on him all of a sudden. He couldn't be sure when exactly it had begun. But of late, he had so often heard her say:

'Let's ask Adam about that, Dick!' or *'I wonder if Adam would teach Mercia to ride; it's high time she began, isn't it?'* It simply had not entered her head that he, Dick, should be the one to teach her. When he suggested it, Tammy had said quietly:

'Well, you know she's a bit nervous of horses, Dick, and you'd only get impatient with her. You teach Richard.'

At the time, he'd not placed a lot of

importance on the conversation, recognising the truth behind Tamily's words. He did become quickly irritated when the child hung back. Mercia had been afraid of the water when he'd taken her down to the stream where he and Tam had bathed so often as kids. He'd finally pushed her in, believing she would get over her nervousness once she felt the delights of swimming in the sparkling, icy-cold water. Instead of which she'd run home screaming and Tamily had been furious. Adam, on the other hand, had the patience of Job and by the end of the summer, Mercia was like a little brown minnow, as much at home in the water as Dick, with whom she played quite happily now she could swim.

Looking back, it struck Dick that Adam played far too big a part in their lives. Both the children were every bit as fond of 'Uncle Adam' as they were of their father. Perhaps the time had come when Tamily, too, was nearly as involved with Bond as with him! She certainly seemed far more relaxed and happy at the weekends when Adam was in and out of the house than when they were alone in the flat. She was always so tense when she was with him and yet he tried every way he knew how to please her.

He looked down at his son, sitting contentedly on Tamily's lap, a small replica of himself. How proud he was of the boy! One day Richard would take over the Allenton estate from him; between now and then, he was going to have so much fun teaching him. They'd ride and swim together as soon as the boy was old enough. He would teach him to play cricket and football, to box and fish and shoot. He'd teach him how to handle a bull and drive a tractor; how to tell a good crop from a poor one. All these things he'd learned from his father as a boy. Although Lord Allenton had never actually done any manual work himself, he'd never objected when Dick had joined the farm workers. He and Tammy had often spent happy hours hay-making, riding home hot and tired and tickling from the grass seeds on top of the haycarts, or riding the old cart horses the tractors had replaced.

The baby turned and stared at him with solemn blue eyes. He looked the very picture of health and intelligence. It was impossible to believe there was anything wrong with him. There was no visible handicap, yet Phelps had confirmed that he was probably deaf. How could such a thing have happened? The child had never been ill; never had a serious fall or bang on his head or ears. His birth, though difficult for Tamily, had been without complications for the child. Dick simply could not believe there was anything wrong.

At the same time, he had to admit that

Richard made no intelligible sounds, only vague noises, some of which sounded like Dad-Dad and yet were not. He was certainly unmoved by sudden noises near him. Dick felt there might well be some other cause than deafness. Maybe the boy had unusual powers of concentration; preferred to continue with his play rather than listen to grown-up talk he was not yet old enough to understand.

'Mr and Mrs Allenton?'

Dick hesitated, unwilling to leave his seat. His reluctance to move forward sprang from his fear of what he was about to be told. Whatever wishful-thinking he might indulge in his instinct warned him that there was indeed something wrong with his son, and at this moment he preferred not to know what it was.

SIX

Tamily walked ahead eagerly, as if she could not wait a moment longer to hear the truth. In her mind she had already accepted that Richard was handicapped and might be for life. Now she wanted to know just how bad that handicap was and just what could be done to help him. Whatever he needed he should have. There was no other thought in her mind.

Wilmot Cosgrave was in his fifties, grey-haired and clean-shaven. He was short, squarely built and a little over-weight. His rather dumpy figure somehow exuded confidence and Tamily liked him instantly. Dick did not. He felt the man lacked the imposing manner he felt suitable for a specialist of Cosgrave's standing. He was obviously well educated, cultured, but he had no bedside manner. After his examination of Richard, he came straight to the point.

'Your son appears to suffer from high-frequency deafness. But I'm happy to tell you he does have some hearing. I suspect there is a certain amount of nerve destruction. Now tell me, Mrs Allenton, did you by any chance have German measles in the early stage of pregnancy?'

Tamily shook her head.

'No, I had all the spotty diseases as a child.'

Mr Cosgrave smiled.

'Well, I asked you because German measles can sometimes cause deafness. There are a lot of other causes, of course, although we don't know as yet what they are. A great deal of research is going on into just this question. Once we know the "why" we can hope to spend our days preventing rather than dealing with the complaint.'

'Right now I'm more concerned with a cure,' Dick broke in sharply. 'Can my son be cured? Can you operate?'

'I'm afraid I can't give you a direct yes or no as yet, Mr Allenton. Sometimes, and I repeat sometimes, an operation can be carried out successfully. But I think it would be wrong of me to raise your hopes at this stage. However, there is quite a lot we know we can do for your son. Fortunately, you have discovered the trouble at an early age. At three or four years old, the problem of teaching him to speak would be greater since he would have passed the stage of automatic vocalising of sound. The main thing now is to improve your son's hearing so that he can learn to talk normally. A great deal has been achieved in the improvement of aids for the deaf and if all goes well it is possible that your boy will learn normal speech and not have the flat monotone of the fully deaf.'

'*Deaf aids?*' Dick's voice was incredulous. 'You're not seriously suggesting we put deaf aids on a kid of this age? Why, that's–'

'Dick, please!' Tamily's hand lay restrainingly on his arm, but he shook it off furiously.

'I'm not going to permit any such thing.'

'Mr Allenton, you don't really have a choice – not unless you wish your child to grow up without speech and I'm sure you don't want that!'

'You said just now it might be possible to operate. If you can't, then someone else can. Whatever's wrong has *got* to be put right.'

Again Tamily tried to intervene but Wilmot Cosgrave, well used to shock reactions from worried parents, shook his head imperceptibly at her and said quietly to Dick:

'Of course we shall arrange an operation if this is possible, Mr Allenton. I merely want you to understand that it might *not* be possible and that, if it is not, there is still a lot we can do to help your son grow up a normal little boy. This would be my aim, as I am sure it is yours.'

Mollified, though still deeply shocked by the idea of Richard in a hearing aid, Dick spoke more calmly:

'Will his hearing improve as he grows older?'

The specialist shook his head.

'I feel that it is best to face facts from the start, Mr Allenton. Fact One is: If it should prove impossible to operate or if such an operation were not a success, then there is no way in which we can help your son's *existing hearing*. But Fact Two is that with the use of a deaf aid, we can vastly improve hearing such as your son's. Fact Three is that with improved hearing it is possible he could acquire near normal use of speech and language.'

For the first time, Tamily spoke:

'Will Richard have to go away? To a special school, I mean.'

'Certainly not for the moment, Mrs Allenton. He needs you, your patience, your love, your understanding. I know you are an intelligent couple' ... he included Dick in his glance ... 'and therefore I intend to be more frank with you than I might be with some other parents. You are going to have to devote a lot of time to your son if you are going to help overcome this handicap. You will need enormous patience, too. Babies are not adults, willing to have deaf aids fixed in their ears without protest. Your son is far too young to appreciate how it can help him. So your first hurdle will be to get him to wear the aid. This can and nearly always does take months.'

'And then?' Tamily prompted eagerly. Many of her worst fears were vanishing now that she had positive action ahead of her; now that this kindly, straight-speaking man was telling her how *she* could help Richard.

'Then you and anyone else in your household must try to keep within close range of him, but this will all be explained to you in detail when the child is fitted for his aid. There will be a teacher of the deaf who will call on you and help you. But I must warn you both that there will be difficulties and setbacks and moments when you feel you are achieving nothing. But if you persevere, then you, his parents, can do a vast amount to help him.'

'You are speaking as if an operation is out of the question,' Dick said sharply. 'Surely it is unnecessary to go into these details about aids and methods of teaching the child if you can cure him in one go with an operation?'

'Mr Allenton, I'm most anxious not to raise your hopes higher than I should. I will need further tests and observations before I can hold out *any real hope* of an operation in your son's case. Even if it were possible, we would certainly not operate while he is so young. Naturally, you are entitled to another opinion if you wish, but I can assure you that this kind of ear condition is one we see all too frequently in this hospital. We do have a special audiology unit here and I do assure you we can offer your child the very best available help!'

'Well, we'll see!' Dick said uncertainly. 'I take it you want to see Richard again so that you can complete your diagnosis?'

'Yes, I will try and fit in an appointment as soon as possible.'

As they turned to go, Mr Cosgrave put a hand on Tamily's arm and said:

'Don't lose heart, Mrs Allenton. Your courage and understanding will be vital factors in this battle.'

In the car going home, Tamily considered his remark. His eyes had been looking deep into hers as if he were speaking to her alone, not to Dick; as if he were somehow speaking about Dick. Poor Dick. He was taking it badly. He was silent and morose, a sure sign that he was worried.

Once back in the flat, he paced up and down the room and finally burst out:

'I'm not at all sure this chap, Cosgrave, *is* the best man. First he says he can operate, then he can't. I don't believe he knows his own mind! It was all if's and maybe's.'

Tamily lifted Richard into his high chair and began to cut up small squares of bread and honey which he stuffed with his usual imperturbability into his rose-bud mouth.

'He never said he could operate on

Richard,' she reminded him quietly. 'Only that it's possible to operate with some forms of deafness.'

'Well, if other people can have operations, why not Richard?' Dick stormed. 'It doesn't make sense to me.'

'I suppose it depends how' ... she hesitated and then spoke out bravely .... 'how bad Richard's ears are. Mr Cosgrave mentioned nerves, didn't he?'

'Damned if I know what he was talking about,' Dick said. 'Silly old idiot burbling on about "courage in battle", as if we were at war or something. I can't say I liked him ... not at all. Not the kind of man I have faith in. His whole attitude was thoroughly pessimistic.'

'I don't agree. I like him,' Tamily began but broke off. There was no point at this stage becoming involved in an argument with Dick over Mr Cosgrave. 'Anyway, we can't judge until he can give us a complete diagnosis. There'll be time enough then to think about another opinion if we don't agree with his findings.'

Dick stood looking down at his son who was paying no attention to his parents' raised voices.

'You talk about time,' Dick burst out, 'but look at him. Look at your son, Tamily. He doesn't hear a word we're saying. How's he going to learn anything if he doesn't pay attention? Seems to me time is the one thing we haven't got. I'm not having any child of mine growing up a deaf mute, I can tell you that.'

It was on the tip of Tamily's tongue to remind Dick that these were Mr Cosgrave's words he was repeating. But she bit back the reminder, knowing that Dick felt the need to blow off steam. But she felt near to tears. His words almost seemed to be a criticism of Richard and this was something he had never done before although the baby had frequently ignored everyone around him in just this same way.

Tamily felt instinctively that it was going to be of the utmost importance to Richard that his parents were at least united in their determination to help him. She must not, no matter the provocation, quarrel with Dick about Richard's treatment. The only important thing was that they both loved Richard and wanted to help him and this they would never be able to do if they were at cross purposes.

'Try not to worry too much about it, darling,' she said gently, sincere in her wish to re-establish understanding with him. The endearment was one she had not used for some time; she used it unconsciously in her efforts to get on better terms with him. He responded at once and came and sat down at the table opposite her.

'It's hard to believe that a couple of days ago we hadn't a worry in the world about the little fellow.' He sighed. 'I just hate to think about it, Tam. Somehow the idea of my son *deaf*. I'd almost rather have him retarded than handicapped this way.'

'Oh, Dick, no! We can help him overcome the deafness and lead a normal life. If he were retarded, he might never be normal.'

'Oh, well, I suppose you're right. All the same, the mere thought is repellent.'

'Then don't think about it,' Tamily said quickly. 'Let's discuss what we're going to do about the future. It's beginning to look as if it's a good thing we are living in London where we are on hand for the best treatment and advice and care for Richard. Would it be terribly disappointing for you if we had to put off our return to Lower Beeches this summer?'

Dick dropped his eyes. This was the moment when he should tell Tamily about his shares; explain that they couldn't go back yet anyway. But he could not do it. One thing he could not face on top of all else was her disillusionment in him. She'd been so proud of the way he'd stood up to his father and made good on his own. He'd really proved to her he was worth something. If he told her he'd gambled all their savings in one mad moment, how could she look up to him again? He told himself she had quite enough to worry about without this news to add to it.

'I suppose we'll have to base our decision on what is best for the boy,' he said. A feeling of guilt made it impossible for him to meet her eyes.

Tamily believed he was trying to hide his disappointment. She felt a rush of genuine gratitude and love for him. It brought her to her feet and round behind his chair where she laid her cheek against his head in the first spontaneous gesture of affection she had shown him in months.

'Oh, Tam!' he said breathlessly. He turned in his chair and drew her against him, so that she was standing between his knees looking down at him.

'Tam!' he said her name again. 'I wonder if you have any idea how much I love you?'

'I love you, too,' she said smiling, her voice soft with tenderness.

'Do you? Sometimes I wonder... I feel–'

'Sssh! Don't let's talk about it,' Tamily said wisely. 'Just believe that I do love you, Dick. I always have done and I always will do. There has never been anyone else for me but you.'

Ignoring the child in his highchair, Dick stood up and put his arms round Tamily and kissed her, at first gently and then with rising passion. This time, Tamily did not try to draw away from him. She wanted to be near him, close to him in spirit and close in thought. That they should be physically close seemed right and necessary.

'I'll put Richard in his playpen,' she whispered.

Dick let her go. He watched her bend over the child, her body young and very slim and yet curiously maternal in its movements. He was no longer worried or unhappy. This was his old Tammy, his warm-hearted passionate girl, his wife, his lover. He'd not found her this way for so long – far too long. His concern for Richard – his worries about his shares were forgotten.

She came back from the nursery and stood in the doorway, her arms at her sides, smiling shyly at him. He drew in his breath sharply and then hurried forward to lead her to their room.

SEVEN

Sandra closed and locked the door of the dairy. She set off across the farmyard to the path through Bluebell Wood which would take her home.

Home was one of the modern cottages on the Allenton estate into which her family had moved when her father was promoted to the position of head cowman just before Sandra, the last of his eight children, was born. That was nearly twenty-one years ago. It wouldn't be long before her father retired and Sandra's eldest brother, Tom, took over as head man. Tom was thirty and knew as much as their father about the herd.

Not all the children had stayed on the estate – some of Sandra's brothers going to work in the town in factories. Two of her sisters were maids up at the Manor House. Sandra herself had never intended to stay on the farm. It had been her ambition since she was a little girl to become a nurse in a children's hospital. She had worked hard at school, obtained a place in a Grammar School and passed all her exams without difficulty. Her family had high hopes for her and it had taken them a long while to get over the shock when she decided at seventeen not to leave home after all.

Sometimes her brothers and sisters teased her about 'young Master Dick', saying she couldn't bring herself to miss the chance of a smile from his bonny blue eyes. But it was only teasing and she took it in good part knowing that the real reason for her remaining at home was still her secret. No one but she knew how desperately in love she was with Adam Bond, the bailiff. She'd been sixteen when he'd first noticed her, standing on the side of the road waiting for the bus to bring her back from school. He'd given her a lift and had put her at her ease for she had been very shy and awkward at that age and blushed easily like most schoolgirls.

Sandra had told herself she would outgrow her secret passion for him. But at seventeen she knew that she never would. If Adam did not want her, she would never marry, although already there were lots of boys around the village asking her for dates.

She acquired a false reputation for being 'snooty' and standoffish. The boys said she thought she was too good for them because she was brainy. But that wasn't the truth. No boy held any appeal for her compared with Adam. Not that he noticed her and she saw him all too seldom. But she never stopped hoping that one day he would talk to her; see that she had grown out of the plump, clumsy schoolgirl stage into a woman; that he might find her attractive and eventually fall in love with her.

She said nothing to her mother who, she knew, would draw attention to the differences in her and Adam's ages. He was half a generation older than she. But that made no difference to the way she felt about him. She loved him. It was that simple and that complicated because he did not seem to know she existed.

Then after Richard's birth she had started to work weekends at Lower Beeches. She had seen Adam regularly. He went often to the house and now he always had a word and a smile for her. These occasions were red letter days in her life. The future no longer seemed so hopeless.

She was not beautiful but she knew that she was attractive. Though tall and well-built, she had long shapely legs, a good figure and wonderful health. She was intelligent, domesticated and well educated. She *could* make Adam a good wife … if he could only need her the way she needed him. But though friendly and polite, he never seemed really to see her except as part of Tamily's household.

Last weekend, Sandra's dreams had received a rude shock. Dick had lost his temper at the breakfast table and accused Tamily of caring more for Adam than for him. Sandra had been appalled, as much shocked by the suggestion of such a relationship as by the fact that Dick could speak in such a way to his wife in front of her.

She tried not to think about it. She told herself the idea of Tamily in love with Adam was absurd; that Tamily had been right to ignore such a silly accusation. But there remained the nagging thought – could Adam be in love with Tamily? If he were, it would explain why he'd never looked around like other men for a wife of his own; why he was so quiet and willing to live the solitary life he did. It would explain why the only time Sandra ever saw him smiling and happy was when he was at Lower Beeches, playing with the children or talking to Tamily.

Of course, Sandra had known for a long time how fond of the young Allenton family Adam was. But that included Dick and the children, especially Richard, his godson. It was ridiculous to imagine Adam was *in love* with Tamily. All the same she could not get the suspicion out of her mind.

Sandra was completely modern in her outlook on life. The fact that she had steadfastly loved one man for nearly five years did not prevent her realising that other people fell in and out of love and that not all marriages were happy ones like her mother's and father's. Marriages did break up sometimes, but not Dick's and Tamily's. Everyone on the estate knew of Tamily's love for Dick. Since she was a tiny girl, she'd heard Tamily spoken of as 'young Master Dick's shadow'. Their wedding had been the most popular event since the end of the war! And not one of Lord Allenton's workers had failed to turn up at the village church and cheer the couple with genuine gladness in their happiness. Somehow Sandra could not bear the thought that such a fairy-tale romance should end any other way than happily-ever-after. She could not and would not believe that Tamily was more than just very fond of Adam. But it was all too easy to believe that Adam loved her for there was no one sweeter, kinder, less selfish than Tamily. Sandra herself was devoted to her and thought her thin, fawn-like face quite beautiful. If she could have chosen to be like anyone else in the world, she would want to be like Tamily. And if *she* thought this, why not Adam, too?

In the cool shade of the wood, Sandra put her hands to her cheeks and felt them burning. Jealousy was a horrible emotion. Yet she knew herself to be jealous and afraid. She had learned to live with the thought that Adam might never love her but she had somehow never faced the fact that he might love someone else.

She remembered the day he had been rushed off to hospital. Everyone had thought he was going blind and she, hating herself for the selfishness of her thoughts, had wondered if this might afford her the opportunity to spend the rest of her life looking after him. He would need someone and she was there, free and able.

Mercifully, he'd been able to go to America and be completely cured. She was glad for him and even glad for herself. Although she had longed for the chance to prove her love to him, his happiness was more important than her own.

To run into him at just this moment in time when her mind was so full of him, caused her to blush furiously as she had not done since she was in her teens.

He greeted her in his usual friendly way.

'Why, Sandra, I thought for a moment you were a ghost in that white dress flickering among the trees.'

'Sorry if I scared you!' Shyness made her curt.

He gave an easy laugh.

'Takes more than a ghost to scare me. On your way home?'

Sandra nodded. She wanted both to escape from him and yet to detain him. She could think of nothing to say.

'Have you seen Jess, by the way?' Adam filled the pause. 'She'd had a telephone call from Tamily to say they had an appointment with the specialist this afternoon. Tamily's ringing again tonight if there's anything more to report.'

'Thank you for telling me, Adam. I've been worrying. Jess didn't come down to the dairy as usual. I expect she was keeping an eye on Mercia.'

Adam pushed his hand through his thatch of dark hair. His face, brown and a little weather-beaten, was worried.

'I do hope something can be done for the boy. This is going to hit Dick pretty hard, too. It's a terrible thing to discover ... that your child is deaf.'

'Not so bad as when you thought you were going blind!' The words were out before she could stop them. Adam raised his eyebrows.

'Well, that's different. I'm old.'

'You're not a bit old. Thirty-something isn't old. Everything is much easier to take when you're young and don't know any different.'

Adam drew out his pipe and began to fill it. He seemed quite willing to stay and talk. With her heart beating furiously, Sandra sat down on the grass. When his pipe was lit, Adam sat down beside her. Patches of sunlight filtered through the trees and lay like warm fingers on her bare legs.

Adam said, more to himself than to her:

'I love that little boy as if he were my own son.'

'Perhaps because you have no sons of your own,' Sandra said softly. 'Haven't you ever wanted your own children, Adam?'

He looked down at her, his expression surprised and slightly amused.

'Just listen to who's talking. From all I hear you've no plans for getting married and raising a family yourself. And not from want of admirers whom you turn down by the dozen.'

'I would get married soon enough – if it were to the right man!' Sandra replied quietly.

Adam looked at her with interest. He'd known her since she was at school and thought her attractive and pleasant as well as very efficient with Tamily's house and children. He'd heard men on the estate mention her from time to time but usually to complain that she was cold and unsympathetic and didn't like men. 'Her heart belies her looks!' one of the young tractor drivers had said sourly.

But the boys were wrong. This girl was obviously saving herself for the right man. He'd be lucky when he came along.

'And what kind of man would you think right?' he asked half-teasing, half-serious.

She turned her face away so that he could not read her expression and for a moment said nothing. Then she murmured:

'An older man... I don't care for boys. Someone who needs a woman to love and care for him the way I'd love and care for the man I loved.'

She turned suddenly and looked directly at him.

'And you, Adam? What kind of woman do you want?'

It was Adam's turn to look down, away from that direct glance of the girl's eyes; eyes that seemed curiously penetrating as if they knew his scent. Could she have guessed that he loved Tamily Allenton? That he'd always loved her? That there never could be another woman he'd feel the same about?

'You're in love with Tamily, aren't you?' The words came out before she could stop them. She raised the back of her hand and held it against her lips, waiting for Adam's angry denial. But when he spoke, it was gently:

'I didn't know anyone had guessed. How did you guess, Sandra?'

She fought against the desire to cry out her anguish at his admission. It was almost more than she could bear to hear him admit he loved Tamily. It was the end of all her hopes, her dreams.

'I don't think I guessed so much as knew, here!' She pressed her hand against her heart. 'It's the way you look at her, perhaps, the way you look after her, maybe; the tone of your voice when you speak to her.'

'And how can you know enough to judge so well when you've never been in love yourself?'

She hesitated. A moment ago, she would

never have dreamt of telling him she loved him. She would rather have died than reveal how she felt. But it didn't matter any more. There could never be anything between them, so she might at least give herself the bitter-sweet pleasure of saying, just once:

'Because I love you, Adam. Because I've been in love with you since I was sixteen. Because I know every bit as well as you do what it's like to be in love. That's why I knew; how I guessed. The way you are with her is the way I'd like to be with you.'

The words came pouring out of her like a cry of pain.

Adam turned on his side and gently, with great tenderness, he rested his hand lightly on her hair. It felt soft and silky and warm beneath his touch.

'I'm so sorry, Sandra. I shouldn't have asked. I never knew. Now we both know each other's secrets.'

She lay beneath his hand, trembling but no longer afraid.

'Don't be sorry,' she said. 'I'm not. I don't think any love, even if it's unrequited, is wasted. It's good to love.'

'What a strange child you are!' Adam said. 'You're right, of course.'

'And you're wrong!' She twisted away from his touch. 'I'm not a child; I am a woman; as much a woman as Tamily.'

Adam remained silent. He knew that he

had hurt her and he hated to see her pain. Life suddenly seemed immeasurably sad. Sandra was young, attractive and, as he'd only just realised, very desirable. Yet he could never love her because his heart was already in Tamily's keeping. It did not matter that Tamily neither knew of it nor cared. But for her, he might have fallen in love with this girl, this woman. Sandra would make a good wife, a good companion; a mother of children. He wanted children very much. Dick's possessive pride in his son had fanned his own sub-conscious desires and he envied him in a way which sometimes hurt with an almost physical ache.

Sandra stood up, straightened her dress, and said:

'Time I went home. Please forget what I said, Adam, just as I shall forget what you told me. As little kids, we used to say Bluebell Wood had a spell on it and magic things happened here. Well, when we next meet, we'll know this conversation never happened and we only dreamt it.'

He let her go, standing watching as she ran away from him for all the world like some woodland nymph. Without her, the wood seemed suddenly chill and friendless; not a place to linger.

He turned away with a sigh and began to walk with slow unhurried steps back along the path from where Sandra had come.

EIGHT

Tamily was happy – as happy as it was possible to be with the thought of little Richard ever in the forefront of her mind. But the problem of the baby's deafness no longer seemed insurmountable because she and Dick were facing it together. It was as if their joint concern for their child had brought them closer than they'd ever been before.

Love was a strange thing, Tamily mused as she wheeled Richard round the park in his pushchair. It wasn't, as she'd once believed, a static thing. It grew, expanded, broadened, widened. Yet she knew, too, that it could go the opposite way and wither, almost die, from neglect. She had neglected Dick in a shameful way. Yet she had not meant to do so. Now all that was past and she could match once more his physical desires with her own. She did not understand how this transformation could have happened. It was true that she had wanted desperately to be close to Dick again. She had recognised the urgent necessity to put their marriage on a sound footing; to return to the early days of their marriage when they had been so happy together. What began as a simple plan to make Dick happy ended with their love-making taking her far, far beyond mere acceptance on her part. Even Richard was momentarily forgotten in their re-discovered joy in one another.

Dick was tender and loving afterwards.

'I thought you'd stopped loving me, Tam. I was beginning to think you'd stopped caring for me and that it would never be like this again. What happened, my darling? What went wrong? I think there were times when you almost hated me!'

She buried her face against his chest and said:

'No, never that. I can't explain it, Dick. It was as if I didn't want to belong to anyone – just to myself. But I couldn't hate you, not really, not deep down inside. I've loved you far too long, Dick, ever to be able to stop loving you!'

Dick smiled happily down at her, his lips touching her hair.

'People say love and hate are akin. Maybe it's true. I think if you were ever unfaithful to me, I'd hate you. I've not such a forgiving nature as yours, Tammy!'

'You know I'd never be unfaithful to you.'

'Not even with Adam?'

'Certainly not with Adam though I can admit now that I do love him, Dick. But it is quite a different kind of love I feel for him.

It's more a tremendous liking. Can you understand that?'

Dick sighed.

'I'm not sure that I can. I'm still a little jealous because he means so much to you. Could you imagine being in love with him, Tam?'

It was on the tip of her tongue to admit she could; that once or twice she had even done so, but an instinctive tact kept her from the admission.

'What is between *us* is something special, Dick, and it has nothing to do with anyone else. I've loved you ever since I can remember.'

'I don't know what I'd do if you stopped loving me, Tam. I need you. I don't think you realise quite how much I do need you. You're all that is good in my life.'

Remembering, Tamily felt a warm glow of happiness. It was good to be needed; good to know that Dick loved her so much. It wasn't just physical love, either. That was only a way of expressing the love they had for one another. It was as if neither could ever touch the very pinnacle of emotion with the other; as if together they were each made more than they could be alone.

A faint smile lingered at the corners of Tamily's mouth as she turned the pushchair in the direction of home. Dick had been so sweet this morning, offering to cut the office again in order to keep her company – prevent her fretting about Richard. He'd kissed her goodbye as if he were going to be away for weeks instead of hours and had promised to telephone at lunch time to enquire if Cosgrave had been able to fix up another appointment for Richard. Tamily was able to tell him that Mr Cosgrave had fixed up for tests to be carried out in the audiology unit at three o'clock the following day.

Dick came home early. He brought with him a bottle of wine and a duck.

'Since I can't take you out to dinner, we'll have a dinner party at home,' he said cheerfully, his arm round her shoulders. 'Then we'll put on some records and dance.'

While Tamily was putting the bird in the oven, Dick went into Richard's room. The boy was lying sleepily in his cot. Tamily heard Dick talking to the baby.

'Don't you worry, old son!' he was saying. 'Your mother and I will see you're fixed up as good as new. A few days in hospital, an operation you'll know nothing about, and you'll be able to hear as well as I can…'

Tamily felt the first shadow fall across the sunshine of her new-found happiness. Obviously Dick was confident Richard's difficulties could be overcome quickly and simply. But from what Mr Cosgrave had told them, they could not count on this. In fact the odds were against Richard being able to

115

have an operation. Dick would be terribly disappointed if the tests showed nothing could be done.

When he rejoined her in the kitchen, she tried gently to tell him so.

'We ought to prepare for the worst in our minds!' she said softly. 'Then it won't seem so bad if–'

'Look, darling, I'm just not going to let myself think about Richard with a deaf aid. Frankly, the very idea appals me.'

Tamily put the potatoes in to roast with the duck and looked up at Dick anxiously.

'Mr Cosgrave did warn us that he might not be able to recommend an operation.'

'Then we'll find someone else who can do it. I'm not taking the first "no" as final. I don't know how you can bear even to think in terms of failure for Richard. I certainly can't.'

'Dick, it isn't failure exactly. So long as he can be given the opportunity to hear and to learn to speak, surely that is three-quarters of the battle? I don't like to think of him in a deaf aid, either – he's so little! But it isn't as if he'd be completely deaf if he has no operation.'

'You sound as if you're resigned to the worst!' Dick said, unbelievingly. 'I just don't see how you can be that way.'

'Isn't it better at least to be aware of the odds and mentally prepared for the worst?'

116

Tamily argued. 'That doesn't mean I'm resigned. All I want is that Richard can live a normal life. We both want that, don't we?'

Dick turned away from her. He didn't want to spoil their present relationship by letting her see how wrong he thought she was to talk in such a way. It was pure defeatism. It was giving up before they'd barely begun.

'You don't seem to understand, Tam. How can any kid's life be normal if he has to go around with wire and boxes and batteries strung all round him? How are the other kids at school going to react? Of course he won't be normal. And you heard what Cosgrave said – Richard will have to learn to talk in a normal voice. He won't even sound like the other children.'

Tamily bit her lip. She understood Dick's reluctance to face the worst but she didn't agree with it at all. He was looking on the gloomier side. If they were going to help Richard, they themselves must believe that a normal life was possible for him. As he grew older and began to understand what it was all about, he'd soon sense it if they, his parents, had doubts about his future. They must be confident if they were going to give him the confidence he would need.

Of course, Dick could be right and an operation might cure Richard completely. But Tamily, much as she wanted to, could not read more hope into the specialist's opinion than he had meant to give them. At the same time, she wasn't certain that it was right to try to belittle any hopes Dick might have.

'Let's not think about it until he's had the tests,' she said gently. 'You may be right, darling. I just pray that you are.'

Dick, too, preferred to let the matter drop. Tamily's pessimistic views, as he thought of them, depressed him and he didn't want to be depressed. He and Tamily had fallen in love all over again and he was happy. He didn't want to think about their child's deformity. It was an ugly word but that was what deafness meant to him – not just a handicap, but a physical deformity. He'd never had a day's illness himself and he had the healthy man's dislike of hospitals and sick rooms. He distrusted doctors and medicines. He never took patent remedies for anything, preferring to let nature take its course if he had 'flu or a cold.

An operation, in Dick's eyes, did not come into quite the same category. If a leg was broken, the bone had to be set. If a chap was going blind, like Bond, then it made sense to let the medical boys operate.

What Dick did not realise was the reason for his pathological dislike of illness and the world of the handicapped. His own adored sister, Mercia, had spent most of her early childhood an invalid. She'd had polio when she was seven and spent a lot of time subsequently in a wheelchair. She had gradually got stronger and eventually been able to walk, though never to ride or dance or join in the sports he so enjoyed. Deep down in Dick's sub-conscious he had hated himself because he had so much preferred to be with Tam, an active little tomboy able to keep up with his pursuits, than to be tied to Mercia's wheelchair.

In fact, Dick was never tied by outside pressures. It was his own love and pity for his little sister which put a moral obligation on him. Naturally kind-hearted, he fought his inclinations to be up and away and spent hours trying to amuse her and keep her happy, refusing ever to acknowledge that his spirit chafed beneath the golden chains of his devotion. As Mercia's health and strength steadily improved, he became less and less aware of those hours of self-sacrifice and now, many years after her death, he remembered nothing but that he had adored her. Only in the deep wells of his sub-conscious did he revert to the past by avoiding anyone who was not completely healthy.

As yet, there were no outward signs of his little son's abnormality. If Dick had his way, there never would be. He wanted Richard operated on and cured and beyond this point he would not allow his thoughts to go. Fear lay beyond that horizon – a fear which he neither recognised nor understood; a fear that Tamily was only just beginning to sense with her strange intuitive understanding of Dick's behaviour.

Whilst the duck was cooking, he and Tamily sat down to a glass of sherry. Dick shared the sofa with her and put an arm round her shoulders. They were at peace with one another. Dick said:

'How thin you are, darling. You must try to eat more.'

Tamily smiled.

'I always was skinny, Dick. I was a skinny little girl and except when I was carrying Richard I've remained that way ever since.'

Dick hugged her, laughing.

'I'm not really complaining. I like my women thin. All the same, darling, I'm sure you've lost weight. As soon as this business of Richard's is sorted out, I'm going to take you away for a really good holiday. Somewhere hot and lazy – Spain, or Greece perhaps?'

'Can we afford it?'

Dick's face clouded.

'We'll manage somehow. Do you realise we haven't been away together alone since our honeymoon? It's all wrong. I want at least two weeks miles from anyone and everyone. I shall probably make love to you all day and every day and you'll come back thinner than ever!'

'Silly!' The smile faded from Tamily's face as she added thoughtfully: 'I don't suppose we'll be able to go this year, Dick. From the way Mr Cosgrave was talking, we're likely to be caught up with Richard for quite a little while.'

Dick's mouth tightened.

'We keep coming back to the same subject, don't we? If Richard has an operation, then it'll all be over quite quickly. He can go down to Lower Beeches to convalesce and Sandra can take over while we go away. You do want to come, don't you, Tam?'

'Of course I do!' Tamily said. 'As if you need to ask! But naturally, we'll have to put Richard's requirements first.'

'Yes, of course!' Dick agreed. But in his own mind, he was simply pandering to Tamily's crazy ideas that Richard couldn't have an operation.

Tamily relaxed. She must stop getting so tense every time she and Dick discussed the baby. Dick was probably quite right to try to be optimistic about his future. All she really wanted to avoid was his disappointment if there could be no operation. Once Dick set his heart on something, he found it so difficult to readjust his ideas. He did not take defeat very well, although when he did give in it was totally and with such good grace that people were completely disarmed. He had been the same as a child. He would argue a point fiercely with his father sometimes for days on end. Finally Lord Allenton would say firmly:

'My mind's made up, Dick. I won't permit it!' and Dick, quite suddenly, would shrug his shoulders, laugh and say: 'Okay, Father. I expect you are quite right!' It had the effect of making people want to give in to him and very often they did.

Tamily knew very well that it had not been easy for someone of Dick's temperament to settle down to marriage. His was a nature that craved constant change and excitement as well as constant action. There had been several girls in his past before he'd woken up to the fact that he loved Tamily far better than any of them! And only once, since their marriage, had he looked at another girl – Carol, whom Tamily tried not to think about. To be fair to Dick, the American girl had been mostly responsible for what had happened. Dick was not the initiator of the affair. It was natural for him to seek and enjoy the company of women; he was attractive to them and they flattered and amused him. But deep down, he loved only her, Tamily, and since Richard's birth he had done everything he could to prove that love. He'd been marvellously patient with her, the more so since patience did not come naturally to him. He was healthy, vigorous and passionate and she knew that it could not have been easy for him to control his nature for so long. She realised this and resolved that she would make it up to him for her past coolness. That it was really past was as much a relief to her as to him.

Dick said it was the doctor's fault for telling him to leave her alone. He was convinced that they could have become lovers again long ago if the doctors had not interfered. Tamily wasn't sure. For months she had dreaded the thought of love-making with Dick. If he had forced himself upon her, she might well have begun to hate him for it. She thought about her extraordinary change of feeling towards him and could not explain it. The mental and the physical were so much inter-related for her that she could not separate them. It did not really matter now, since they were happy together again. The only important thing was that they should stay this way. She had hated those months of isolation from him. They were like young sweethearts who had quarrelled, nearly lost one another and suddenly been reunited.

In her present mood of relaxed contentment, Tamily, like most women, longed to spread her happiness amongst those around her. She thought of Adam, alone so much of the time, and said suddenly:

'You know, Dick, Adam ought to get married. He's so fond of children and so good with them. He ought to have some of his own. Don't you agree?'

'Perhaps he doesn't want to be tied down to a nagging wife!' Dick grinned down at her.

'Seriously, darling, don't you think we ought to try and find someone for him?'

Dick laughed.

'You've enough to do without match-making,' he said. 'Anyway, if Bond wants a wife, there's one on his doorstep ... a pretty one, too.'

Tamily looked at him wide-eyed.

'You don't mean Sandra?'

'And why not?' Dick finished his sherry, put down his glass and hugged Tamily to him. 'She's young and she's pretty. I admit she is a little plump for my liking, but I should have thought she'd suit Adam very well.'

Tamily sighed.

'I just never thought of it. I know Sandra likes him.'

'But he's too busy paying court to you to notice her!' Dick said shrewdly and not without a tinge of jealousy. 'Mind you, I can see his point – with you around, the poor girl doesn't stand much of a chance. And don't look so horror-stricken. You can't help being so much more attractive.'

But Tamily wasn't so sure. She'd never refused the time and friendship Adam offered her. Now, seeing the situation through Dick's eyes, she realised that she had been very selfish. She had needed Adam in a way she found hard to define. He was her one stable rock to cling to when her marriage had seemed to go on the rocks. He was always there in the background, loving in his strange, silent way; helping unobtrusively just by offering that stability. But she'd been selfish to take anything from him when there was nothing she could give him in return.

'Forget it, darling!' Dick said. 'He's just a slow mover, that's all. He'll wake up one of these days and propose to the girl. It's not your worry. I'm your worry. For instance, right now I'd like to be kissed. I'm feeling lonely and unwanted!'

She looked into his laughing eyes and a smile came into her own.

'You'll just have to go without – the duck will be burning!' she said. But she made no real effort to escape from him and allowed him to draw her back down beside him.

'Sometimes'... said Dick breathlessly as he kissed her between each word ... 'I don't feel married to you at all!'

'Funny kind of compliment, that is!' Tamily whispered, and then words were forgotten as his lips came down on hers once again.

NINE

'Well, how did it go?'

Dick sat down on the arm of Tamily's chair and kissed her on the cheek. She was looking flushed, almost excited and he believed she must have good news for him about Richard.

'Dick, it's a wonderful hospital!' she burst out. She had been waiting an hour for him to return home so that she could tell him all about her afternoon visit. 'I've never seen so much up-to-date equipment and efficiency in my life. And Dick, Mr Cosgrave was there most of the time. He's obviously taking a personal interest in Richard. I wonder if it's because Richard is Phelps' patient? You were absolutely right to insist we came back to London. I'm sure he wouldn't have given us nearly so much attention if we'd come through poor old Dr Timms.'

Dick was pleased and flattered.

'Tell me the rest, I'm all ears!' he said, putting an arm round her shoulders.

'Well, we went to the audiology unit – I'll never be able to say that word properly! Richard had a long session with a psychologist which he seemed to enjoy; then the audiologist – he's a sort of head man of the

126

unit – he checked Richard's hearing ability. Then the two of them and Cosgrave had a conference and they took an impression of Richard's ears. Mr Cosgrave said it would only be a couple of days before I can take Richard for a fitting.'

'Fitting? Fitting for what?' Dick's voice was toneless.

'Well, for his hearing aid,' Tamily said, suddenly hesitant.

Dick got up and walked quickly away from her. He deliberately turned his back on her so that she could not see how hard he was fighting to control his temper. At all costs, he must not fly off the handle. It was important he didn't antagonise her now they were getting on so well again.

'Look, Tam,' he said with a great effort at casualness. 'I know you're anxious to help Richard and so am I, but at the same time, I've said all along, I'm NOT willing for him to have a hearing contraption strung round his neck.'

Tamily's face whitened. She clasped her hands together and tried to keep calm. Mr Cosgrave had warned her that she might have to face a certain amount of resistance from Dick. She ought to have had more tact than to blurt it out in so sudden a fashion, but she had genuinely put all thoughts of an operation out of her mind from the moment Cosgrave had told her it was out of the

127

question. She should have remembered Dick's parting words when he went off to work this morning. 'Let's hope this afternoon brings some news about an op for young Richard.'

'Darling, I'm sorry! I should have explained first what Mr Cosgrave said. Come and sit down and I'll tell you.'

But Dick, though he turned round to face her, remained where he was, leaning against the table by the window, half sitting on his hands. The lines of his face were taut – unrelaxed.

'Well, what did he say?'

'It isn't the *best* of news but at least it isn't in any way hopeless,' Tamily said soothingly. 'Apparently the nerves in Richard's ears are damaged. Cosgrave doesn't know why although he seems inclined to think it may be due to drugs I took when Richard was on the way. And as it is the nerves which have been affected, there just isn't a hope for an operation.'

'That's just his opinion!' Dick's voice was sharp. 'As I said the other day, we can go to someone else who may have a different idea about it.'

Tamily frowned.

'But, darling, any specialist we see would say the same thing. There isn't any doubt about it being damaged nerves causing the deafness.'

'What you're really saying is that Cosgrave and this audiologist fellow don't doubt it, yet you have already admitted they aren't sure what caused the trouble, so how are they so certain what the trouble is?'

Tamily fought against the desire to raise her voice in exasperation. As quietly as she could, she explained:

'It isn't quite the same thing, is it, darling? They believe the drugs were responsible but they can't prove it. But they have proved to themselves that the nerves in Richard's ears aren't working properly.'

'They've proved it to themselves and apparently to you, but not to me. I'm sorry, Tam, but I'm just not satisfied.'

'Oh, Dick, if only you'd been there with me. You must ring up Mr Cosgrave and let him explain. Honestly, darling, everything he said made sense. And the audiologist was in complete agreement. I don't think we can doubt them.'

'Well, *I* doubt them!' Despite his intentions, Dick's temper flared up. He wasn't going to have Richard written off so easily, for that's what it would mean. Tamily was prepared to believe anything she was told, but not he, Dick.

He went over and sat down beside her.

'Look, Tam!' he said more quietly. 'Look at it for a moment from Richard's point of view. Can you honestly say the child won't mind wearing a deaf aid? Of course he will. You can't really want him to remain handicapped all his life?'

'Darling, of course I don't, you know that. But the facts are he *is* handicapped. He is partially deaf and without an aid he's never going to learn to talk or to understand what we say. That's a much worse handicap than the mere fact of wearing a deaf aid. I don't think he'll mind. He was as good as gold today – he didn't seem to bother when they poked around his head and ears. He never cried once.'

'Why should he? Presumably no one hurt him. That isn't the point. The point is, we've got to find someone who will operate and put things right.'

'But, Dick, you can't replace damaged nerves. Mr Cosgrave said so.'

'Well, we'll see!' Dick said. 'First thing tomorrow, I'm ringing up Phelps to put me on to another ear, nose and throat specialist. There must be others. Who's the head man at Guy's, at Thomas's, at Great Ormond Street? I'll see them all if I have to but I'm not giving up until I've seen the last one. Then, if necessary, I'll take Richard to America.'

'You can't seriously mean that, Dick? By all means let's have a second opinion – Guy's or Great Ormond Street – the best Phelps can suggest. But if he confirms Cosgrave's diagnosis, then we have to accept it.'

'You already have accepted it,' Dick said shrewdly. 'You've even allowed them to take an impression of Richard's ears, all ready for a deaf aid.'

Tamily drew in her breath.

'It didn't occur to me you'd react in this way,' she said. 'The important thing seemed to be to start Richard hearing as quickly as possible. The longer we delay, the more difficult it is going to be to teach him to talk. Time's important to him, Dick. I thought you'd understand that just as I did.'

'I can understand well enough what is important,' Dick replied coldly. 'It's important that he should be completely normal – cured for good and all. That's my aim for Richard – not a permanent life-time handicap.'

Tamily remained silent. There was nothing more she could think of saying that would change Dick's viewpoint. He seemed to be obsessed with the idea of an operation and was refusing to accept what she already felt in her heart was inevitable. If Mr Cosgrave or the audiologist had been able to give her any hope, however faint, of an outright cure, then she would be as Dick now was, ready and anxious not to leave one single stone unturned until they found someone to provide a complete cure. But there was no hope – none at all.

She thought miserably of the drugs she

131

had taken which were the possible cause of all this trouble. If only she had known! But Mr Cosgrave had said she must never blame herself.

'You are no more to blame than the mothers who took thalidomide believing it to be perfectly safe,' he had said. 'You must never blame yourself, Mrs Allenton. Just try not to think about what is past. The important thing now is the future and to help your little son to as near normal a life as possible!'

As if aware of her train of thought, Dick said suddenly:

'What drugs was that man referring to, anyway? I don't remember you taking anything before Richard was born?'

'But I did, Dick. It was when…' She broke off suddenly and looked away from him, her eyes uneasy.

'When, what? Is this something I don't know about? What's been going on, Tamily? You've got to tell me.'

'But it isn't important. We don't even know if it was the drugs which–'

'I want to know, Tam. *When did you take drugs and what drugs?*'

She looked up at him then and met his gaze.

'If you have to know, Dick, I'll have to tell you. It was when you and Carol … well, I suppose my nerves were on edge and Dr Timms gave me a prescription for something that he said would help me. I don't know what it was exactly but Mr Cosgrave seemed to think it could have been one of the drugs they are only now realising can cause damage to an unborn child.'

Dick stood looking down at his wife, more deeply shaken than Tamily realised. So all this was his fault. He had made Tamily so ill with worry that she'd been forced to take something she would never otherwise have needed. *He* was the original cause of Richard's deformity. The thought was unbearable; intolerable.

Seeing his expression, Tamily ran to him.

'Don't let's think about the past, Dick. It isn't important. Cosgrave didn't know it was the drugs I took which harmed Richard. Oh, darling, don't please start blaming yourself. Cosgrave told me we must never do that. It was an accident – just an accident.'

Gently, without anger, Dick detached himself from her arms. He looked suddenly older and for the first time in his life, strangely cynical.

'You said just now we had to face facts. Well, I'm facing the fact I'm probably responsible for Richard's deafness. I made your life hell when you were carrying him and so you had to take some filthy medicine to keep you from going round the bend. I wonder how you can even bear to look at me, Tam.'

'Dick, I *love* you. Don't you understand? This doesn't make any difference to the way I feel about you. I love you! You're my husband and Richard's father and I love you.'

'Some husband! Some father!' Dick said bitterly. 'Well, you can't dislike me more than I'm disliking myself right now. My God, if ever a man had to pay for his sins!'

Tamily caught his arms and began to shake him in her anxiety not to let him continue in this vein. She could not bear to hear him abuse himself in this fashion.

'Stop it, Dick. You've nothing at all to blame yourself about. Cosgrave said there are hundreds of children born every year with imperfections of some kind or another which no one can account for. Richard might be one of them. He only asked about the drugs because he's interested in the causes of deafness for some research work he's doing.'

Dick shrugged his shoulders.

'So you are just too nice, too kind, too loving to want to believe the worst,' he said quietly. 'But that doesn't alter the way I feel about myself. Now let's forget it and find something else to talk about. I'm sick of Cosgrave's name and I don't want to hear another word about deaf aids. Let's have a drink. I could do with one.'

'They're on the table!' Tamily replied. 'But will you go and say good night to Richard first? He's probably almost asleep by now.'

Dick turned towards the door, hesitated and then came back.

'If he's asleep, I won't disturb him. I expect he's tired after all the excitement. Well, what are you going to have, Tam? Sherry or something stronger?'

Tamily caught her lower lip between her teeth. Perhaps she was being over-sensitive and misjudging Dick, but she could not stop herself wondering why he wasn't going to see the child. The good-night ritual never varied when he was home at bedtime. Even if Richard were asleep, Dick always looked in on the children. Why not tonight? *Why not tonight?*

'Don't stop loving him!' she thought. 'Don't feel guilty about him! Even if you were indirectly responsible for his being deaf, he won't ever know or care. He needs you to go on loving him just as I need you to go on loving me. Don't turn your back on us!'

Dick came across the room and handed her a drink. Then he sat down opposite her and said:

'Since this seems to be the night for bad news, I might as well confess that I have some for you, too. Want to hear?'

Something in his tone of voice – a

flippancy – made her realise that what he had to say was more serious than his opening remark suggested.

She nodded.

'It's about our finances!' Dick said in a flat monotone. 'I'd made up my mind not to tell you but you'll have to know sooner or later so why not now? The fact is, I've made a damn silly mistake. I put a lot of money into some shares which have taken a very nasty knock. Do you understand? I've chucked a few thousand pounds of our hard-earned savings down the drain!'

She stared at him unbelievingly.

Dick gave a short laugh.

'Don't look so stunned!' he said. 'You ought to know by now that you married a good-for-nothing half-baked idiot.'

'Don't talk like that, please!' she broke in. 'If you've had some bad luck...'

'Not bad luck. It was just plain bad judgement,' Dick interrupted. 'So you see, Tam, we can't start farming Lower Beeches this year, after all. I'm sorry.'

'Oh, Dick, I'm sorry, too!' There was no recrimination in her voice, only a genuine regret. She was still not willing to believe that he had wantonly thrown the money away. Dick had been saving too hard and too long for that. He wanted to go back to Lower Beeches every bit as much as she did. This was as big a blow to him as to her.

'Yes, I thought you would be. Not much I can say, is there, except to repeat that I'm sorry.'

'Darling, don't please worry about it. The way things are with Richard, we probably couldn't go back now even if we wanted to.'

She hesitated to add that she had been told she might be visited more often by the teacher of the deaf here in London than if she lived in a remote country area. There was a shortage of such teachers and help of this kind was invaluable. But until Dick would accept that Richard must have a deaf aid, she couldn't console him with this information.

'Thanks for not bawling me out!' Dick said into the silence. 'It's what I should have expected from you, Tam. You know, don't you, that you're far too decent a person to be married to someone like me. I just can't match up to your goodness.'

'Don't, Dick. It isn't true and you know it. I'm inadequate in lots of ways – just not in the same way as you, that's all.'

'*You've* never been unfaithful to *me*.' It was a statement of fact.

'No, but then I didn't have the same opportunity or temptation, otherwise I might have been unfaithful.'

'Somehow I don't think so!'

Hoping to joke him out of this mood, Tamily said:

'Yet only the other day you were accusing me and Adam of all kinds of things.'

Dick did not return the smile.

'Maybe you should have left me – married him,' he said. 'He'd make a good husband.'

'Darling, I don't want Adam, I want you. I'm perfectly happy with the husband I have, thank you very much. I don't know how we come to be talking like this, but it's just plain silly. Nothing has happened to stop me loving you. I don't know a lot about shares but I do know they fluctuate and it isn't a crime because you bought some which went down instead of up.'

'Tammy, I shouldn't have bought them in the first place. They were a gamble and I'd no right to gamble with money I look upon as *ours,* for our future.'

'All right, so you gambled and lost. You don't think I am going to stop loving you and wanting to be married to you because of that?'

Suddenly he was beside her, his arms round her, crushing her against him.

'God, I do love you so much!' he cried. 'I know I don't deserve you but I couldn't let you go. I need you, Tam. I love you.'

She looked up at him, at the unhappy blue eyes and the quiff of fair hair that curled down on his forehead so like Richard's. This man was her lover but he was also her child. She stroked his head and spoke to him soothingly, as she would to Richard, and gradually the tenseness seemed to leave his body; the tight lines about his mouth to soften.

'Nothing matters as long as we go on loving each other!' she whispered.

But even as he bent to kiss her soft red mouth, Dick felt that this time he could not so easily forget his worries. The past lay like a dark shadow on his happiness, reminding him of his guilt, his unfaithfulness to Tamily, the hurt he had inflicted on her and, because of it, the irreparable damage he had done to his son. It was something he knew he could never forget. Tamily might be able to forgive him but Dick could not envisage a time, unless Richard was completely cured, when he would forgive himself.

TEN

The week, which had begun so hopefully for Tamily, ended in disaster. True to his word, Dick refused to accept Mr Cosgrave's diagnosis and called in a Harley Street specialist who did a great deal of work at Great Ormond Street. It was a long, painful interview in which the new man confirmed Cosgrave's findings and told Dick that he could not have placed his child in better hands. He could do nothing more for Richard than was already being done.

From that moment on, Dick refused to have Richard's deafness mentioned in conversation. Tamily could not understand his reactions. If he now accepted that Richard would have to wear a deaf aid and that an operation was out of the question, why was he refusing to discuss it openly?

'Dick, we *have* to talk about Richard's treatment?' Tamily said on the Friday when Dick for the third time refused to look at the deaf aid she had been given at the hospital that morning.

'We don't seem able to talk about anything else, do we?' Dick's voice was sarcastic.

'Darling, don't be like that,' Tamily

140

pleaded. 'I know you hate the idea of an aid for Richard but we haven't any alternative, have we? And since he has to wear one, you and I will have to help him. At the moment, he's resisting it violently.'

'Can't say I blame him!' was Dick's curt reply. 'Nor am I in the least surprised. He's far too young for anything of the kind.'

Instinct warned her not to become involved in any arguments about Richard, but she tried to get Dick to admit that the experts must know what they were doing. If other toddlers could be made to wear aids, then so could Richard. But Dick, though he listened with a studied politeness, merely replied:

'Well, it's up to you, Tam. Personally, I haven't the least intention of trying to force the boy to put that damn thing on. I'd be a hypocrite if I did since I think this is all a lot of nonsense. You do what you please, but don't expect me to become involved. I'd rather not hear the sordid details!'

Tamily was near to tears. Try as she might, she could not understand Dick's ostrich-like behaviour. It seemed to her both childish and selfish. They should both be thinking only of Richard.

To her dismay, Dick's strange behaviour intensified. He announced that he wasn't going down to Lower Beeches that weekend.

'Not going?' Tamily echoed, stunned. 'But

we always go every weekend. And besides, we haven't seen Mercia all week. She'll be expecting us. I told Mother we'd be down for lunch tomorrow. Everything will be prepared.'

'You go if you want. I've no intention of spending my weekend listening to you and Mother and Father and Jess all on about Richard. You can do your nattering without me.'

Tamily put out her hand in a gesture of appeal.

'Dick, don't talk like that. You know I don't want to go without you. Anyway, what would you do up in London? It's going to be warm – the forecast is good. I promise we won't natter on about Richard if that's all that's worrying you.'

Dick half-turned towards her.

'Then let's you and I go away somewhere together; just the two of us, Tam.' The tension left his face and he looked eager as he warmed to his own idea. 'We can leave Richard with Jess and Sandra and we'll drive off to the coast, stop where we find a place we like. How about it, darling? It would be fun and you deserve a break.'

Tamily hesitated. In one way she would love to go off alone with Dick. They were so seldom alone and it would do them both good. But at the same time she felt certain that it would be wrong to go this particular weekend. The audiomatrition who had fitted Richard's deaf aid had told her:

'Keep persevering with it, Mrs Allenton. Don't be angry or irritable when he pulls it out – just wait an hour or two and then try again. When he does leave it in, keep within close range of him – it works best at close range: and always keep in front of him so that he can see your lip movements. Make sure that the light shines on your face so that he can see your mouth. Lip reading is important for him so that he can associate the sounds he hears with the movement of your mouth.'

No, she couldn't go away and leave Richard now, just when his training was beginning. Surely Dick would understand?

But Dick did not. He openly admitted his resentment that she should put Richard before him, refusing to allow that these were special circumstances and that he was acting selfishly. Tamily's desire not to make an issue of it was lost in one of her rare outbursts of temper:

'You're completely self-centred, Dick. You always were. You should be thinking of Richard now, not yourself.'

Dick made no effort to control his own temper.

'Go on, then, why don't you say it? Say what you're really thinking – that it was my fault you had to take those drugs and therefore my fault Richard is deaf.'

'Dick!' Her temper cooled at once. She was now only concerned with the wrong impression she had somehow imparted to him. 'Of course it isn't your fault ... anyone's fault. I've never once suggested that it was.'

'Didn't you? Just now you said I was completely self-centred and always had been. What was that supposed to mean?'

Tamily drew a deep breath, trying to remain calm.

'Just exactly what I said and no more, Dick. You are thinking of what you want and not what Richard needs. Of course I would far rather be going off somewhere with you this weekend but how can I go now? I have to try to get Richard used to wearing his aid. Mr Cosgrave as well as the audiologist impressed on me the need to get him started as soon as possible. Surely that isn't so hard to understand?'

But Dick was beyond understanding. He had still not recovered from the shock of being told quite definitely and finally that Richard couldn't have an operation. Somehow, since the first meeting with Cosgrave, he'd managed to convince himself that the man knew nothing and a better man would tell him Richard's trouble could be overcome. He'd wanted it so much he'd willed himself into believing it was possible. Now he had no alternative but to accept the truth that his son was to remain handicapped for life and he could not bear the thought. Even to see the white cardboard box in which the apparatus lay turned his stomach and made him feel physically ill. And behind everything lay the horrible awareness that this was all the result of his unfaithfulness to Tamily. No matter how she might argue otherwise, or deny that the drugs she took were responsible, he knew deep down inside him that it had to be this. It was a just retribution for his sins. *The sins of the fathers shall be visited upon the children...*

'I don't want to talk about it any more. You go down to Lower Beeches and see Mercia by all means but I'm not coming with you. I'll probably go and watch some cricket at Brighton.'

'You don't mean that, Dick?' Her voice was miserable and unhappy. It seemed to reproach him. He said:

'What's the matter? Don't you trust me to behave myself if you aren't there to keep an eye on me?'

Tamily turned and left the room. She was bitterly hurt and very worried. Somehow she felt sure that she had mismanaged Dick; that she was responsible for the extraordinary attitude he was taking about Richard. She must have advice. They couldn't go on this way. Perhaps her mother could help her.

But Jess had no helpful suggestions.

'Obviously he feels guilty about Richard, but I don't think it will last, Tamily. You know Dick can't stay bad-tempered and irritable for long. Give him a little time to get used to the idea and I'm sure he will come round.'

Tamily did not mean to take her marital problems to Adam but somehow it all came pouring out when he asked her, as was inevitable, why Dick had not come down with her.

'Poor Tamily, you are having a time of it!' he said, when she had explained Dick's strange behaviour.

Without warning, Tamily burst into tears. Even as the tears dripped down her cheeks, she thought how silly it was that she could control herself with Dick and yet her self-control gave way beneath Adam's warm sympathy.

'The worst part of all is that he won't take any notice of Richard!' she said in a small choked voice. 'Oh, Adam, you don't think this can alter the way he loves Richard, do you? Dick's always been so tremendously proud of him and I just couldn't bear it if he rejected him now when Richard needs him most.'

Adam resisted the impulse to take her in his arms and kiss away the tears. If his love could have helped her, he would have given it unstintingly but he knew that it wasn't his love she needed now – it was Dick's. If only Dick would grow up! he thought bitterly. He was the eternal boy, demanding Tamily's devotion and support but giving her none in return. How could he be so insensitive! But he said nothing of this to Tamily.

'Of course Dick won't turn against his own son. How could any man! He's just suffering from shock, I expect. By the time you go back tomorrow, he'll be in a different mood altogether.'

Tamily blew into Adam's handkerchief and sniffed, trying to smile.

'I hope you're right. All the same, Adam, I can't help thinking that *you* wouldn't have reacted this way. Why, you spent all the morning trying to encourage Richard to wear that horrible aid. Do you know, I'm almost beginning to hate the thing as much as Dick. I can see it's going to need endless patience.'

'The kind of patience I know you have in plenty!' Adam said. 'You must never lose heart, Tamily. For Richard's sake as much as for your own – and Dick's.'

She nodded. Adam, at least, was on her side.

'I know you're right. I'm just being silly. Forgive me. I expect I'm going all the wrong way about this. I'm over-anxious to succeed and yet I've been warned it can and usually does take months to persuade a baby to

147

keep a deaf aid in place. I suppose I've talked myself into thinking Richard will be different and I'll have him hearing and talking overnight. Of course that's silly. Mr Cosgrave said Richard would probably object to it, and if he did it would be best to wait a day or two and then try again.' Adam, all too conscious of her nearness, of the touch of her arm alongside his own, moved casually away from her.

'You should have gone away with Dick for the weekend as he suggested,' he said with difficulty, knowing that in his heart he was glad she was here; asking for his help; needing his sympathy. He hated himself for the thought. Tamily belonged to Dick and he must never make the mistake of forgetting it.

'I don't know what I'd do without you!' Tamily said, unaware of the bitter-sweet taste her words had for him. 'I expect you'll laugh, Adam, but do you know Dick's quite jealous because he knows I depend so much on you. In a way, he's quite right. You're the most wonderful friend to me, and I do depend on you. I feel better just for talking it all over with you.'

They were alone in the garden of Lower Beeches. Sandra had taken the children up to the Manor House for tea with their grandparents. Tamily was going up later to collect them. She had had such a blinding headache she had welcomed the thought of a quiet afternoon in a deckchair under the beech trees where it was cool and shady.

There Adam had found her, depressed and alone, and had remained to try and cheer her up. Now he was suddenly very conscious of their solitude. He knew it to be dangerous. Tamily spoke innocently of her need for him but he knew he was not innocent in his need for her. He loved her desperately and hopelessly. This in itself was nothing new, but the situation was changing. He could not stop the thought racing through his mind that if Dick persisted in this attitude, his marriage to Tamily could founder. Tamily was a devoted and adoring mother. It was only natural that all that was most maternal in her should rush to protect a child she now knew to be handicapped. Dick would have to understand this reaction and stand back, take second place. But would he? *Could* he? If he did not, then Tamily would put Richard's needs first without question.

'You're very quiet, Adam! I'm always so selfish when I'm with you. I talk about myself and my problems but never about yours. What have you been doing all the week, Adam? Yours is such a solitary life, isn't it? Do you know, Dick and I were saying the other night that we thought you ought to get married.'

Adam forced himself to laugh; to make

light of her remark.

'Great Scott! Whoever to?' he asked.

Tamily smiled.

'Well, what about Sandra? I'm sure she's in love with you. She goes pink every time your name is mentioned.'

'Sandra's only a child – years younger than I am!'

'She's no child, Adam – she's very much a woman. Is there no chance you could fall in love with her?'

It was on the very tip of his tongue to say: 'No, it isn't possible because I'm in love with you!' But he bit back the words, unhappily aware that if this conversation went on much longer, he would lose what little self-control he had and blurt out the truth.

Looking at him, seeing his head turned away from her, the strong sunburnt hands twisting restlessly in his lap, Tamily suddenly realised why he sat so silently, unable to find the right words to answer her. She ought not to have mentioned the word love to him. She never thought about it consciously but deep in her sub-conscious she knew that Adam still loved her. It had been childish and thoughtless of her to disregard the enduring quality of his feelings; to tell herself that that phase of the past was over and finished. Adam was not the kind of man to love easily or lightly.

She thought back to the past and the memory of Adam declaring his love for her was tinged with horror at the thought of what had provoked the situation. She and Dick had quarrelled violently in front of Adam, in his house. Furiously hurt by Dick's admission of his affair with Carol, she had tried to hurt him by telling him she and Adam were in love. After Dick had left, Adam had confessed that it was, in fact, quite true that he loved her. At that time, he'd believed he was going blind and because he had no hope of recovery, he had nothing to offer her if she left Dick. By the time they all knew his sight could be restored, she and Dick were reconciled and he had never mentioned his feelings again. After Richard's birth, he had started to visit Lower Beeches once more both as a friend and as Richard's godfather and it was as if that scene had never taken place.

Tamily pushed the memory to the back of her mind, fearing it might destroy the friendship between her and Adam – a friendship she treasured deeply. She turned to him now, distressed by her thoughts:

'Adam, sometimes you must come near to hating me. I have been a poor friend to you, haven't I? I take and take from the storehouse of your kindness and understanding and there is so little I can give you in return.'

He leant forward and caught her hand in

his. His eyes looked into hers with a burning intensity.

'It is enough for me that we are friends, Tamily. I am happy if you are happy. If I can help you then I feel I've earned the right to your friendship. That's all I ask. As to you giving me so little – you have given me a godson, the nearest thing to a son of my own. You know how I love Richard, what he means to me. So you see, the benefits are not one-sided.'

Tamily left her hand in his. His touch was strangely comforting. She sighed and then suddenly smiled.

'You have a wonderful way of making everything seem right, Adam. A moment ago I felt guilty and now I don't. I suppose what is between us *is* rather strange, isn't it? You mean more to me than anyone else I know outside my family. Do you think it's unusual that we can keep a platonic friendship that is so precious to us both and yet does no harm to anyone else?'

Adam let her hand fall. He lay back in his chair, his eyes closed against the question Tamily had asked him. Of course, it wasn't really a platonic friendship. She must know that, too. He loved her. But for Dick, she might even have fallen in love with him, Adam. But Dick existed – had always existed as far as Tamily was concerned – and no matter how stormy their marriage, she still loved him. She might hate him at times; but she could never be indifferent to him. This kind of loving was more compulsive than voluntary. Something in Dick attracted Tamily in a strange irresistible way. The bond between himself and Tamily was born of a different kind of love. It had in it respect and kindness; liking, sympathy and an innate understanding of the other's thoughts and feelings. They were not opposite, as Tamily and Dick were opposite. Their thoughts and reactions were those of but one single person.

Theirs might have been the perfect marriage, Adam thought. There would be no stress, no tension, no sacrifice, no need to adapt one nature to another. But it would lack the exciting tempest of loving; the flashes of brilliance as two opposing forces met and flamed into one. Because of this, he could never measure up to Dick in Tamily's eyes, and, even if he could forget that, loyalty to the Allenton family forbade him ever trying to take Dick's wife from him.

Not for the first time Adam found himself wondering if it would not be best for Tamily, for himself and for Dick if he cut completely away from the Allentons. Only by doing so, by making a complete break, could he hope to stop thinking in terms of what might have been. It was, he told himself, wrong to live on dreams. He should do as Tamily said and

153

get married, have a family of his own.

He thought of Sandra and sighed. She was a sweet girl; quiet, thoughtful and yet with a sense of humour which appeared on all too rare occasions. When she laughed her large blue eyes would sparkle and her soft red mouth widen into a generous smile. He enjoyed her company which was natural and unspoiled. Like himself, she was close to nature, understanding the ways of the wild. She would make a good wife. Moreover, she loved him. She had told him so.

There was only one snag, Adam thought, sighing. He did not love her. His heart was all too firmly in Tamily Allenton's keeping.

ELEVEN

Dick did not enjoy the cricket. Runs came slowly and he found he wasn't in the least interested in the game. At the back of his mind, he knew he didn't really want to be here at all. He wanted to be at Lower Beeches with Tamily.

'Idiot!' he told himself. He'd only just managed to sweep away one barrier between them when he had promptly erected another. He should have been more understanding about her wish to stay with Richard this weekend. He had behaved first like a jealous schoolboy because she gave the child preference; then been too proud to retract his threat to spend the weekend in Brighton of all places!

He decided to go home. If he drove back to London this evening, packed a suitcase and set off at once for Lower Beeches, he could be there by midnight. He would surprise Tamily and all would be well between them again.

But in the car driving swiftly up the wide double road, he began to doubt whether in fact 'all would be well'. There was still the problem of Richard to be solved. He wasn't at all sure how he was going to deal with the situation. What he would really like to do would be to take the boy over to America where there might be advanced techniques for an operation for deafness. He couldn't afford the trip, of course, but his father might subsidise him if he thought it was for Richard's good. But would he? His father thought him, Dick, a 'harum scarum' and always sided with Tamily. The old man thought the world of her. If Tamily convinced him Richard should wear a confounded aid, his father would back her all the way. If only there was one medical opinion to support his belief that there was someone somewhere who could put Richard right. The two specialists were adamant and even he felt it was pointless getting a third opinion in England.

Dick pulled the car up outside a small, attractive-looking pub. He could do with a drink while he thought out his next move. The place looked inviting and cheerful. He wandered into the bar and ordered a brandy. The drink improved his mood. He looked around him to find an attractive red-haired woman sitting by the window, staring at him over the top of her cocktail glass.

Dick was well used to such looks from women. This one was unescorted, thirty-five-ish, chic. Judging by her clothes, she obviously had plenty of money. She did not drop her eyes at his scrutiny but allowed herself a slight smile, Dick smiled back. He could never resist a pretty woman. He turned away to order another drink. When he looked round again, she was standing by his elbow.

'Would you pass the olives, please?' The smile was still in her eyes and there was little doubt it was meant for him. Dick slid off the bar stool and passed the saucer of olives. She took one and nibbled it between small, white teeth. Her eyes were wide-apart and very green, the nose delicate and Grecian in shape. The pink silk jersey dress clung to her figure which was well-rounded but not fat.

'Helga von Routenhahn!' she said, holding out a small hand with long, pink-tipped nails. Her voice had a slight accent Dick could not place.

He introduced himself and she slid on to the stool beside him.

'I was just beginning to get a little bored!' she told him. 'Now I am not bored and I would like another martini!'

Dick grinned. A mild flirtation wouldn't hurt anyone and obviously this woman was trying to pick him up. He, too, was a little bored.

'You're not English. French, perhaps?'

She shook her head.

'No, Hungarian. You, of course, are English!'

While she sipped her drink, Dick learned more about her. She was the widow of a North country industrialist who had left her with a lot of money and time on her hands. For years she had kept busy entertaining on a lavish scale for her husband's business friends. It was not long after he died before she became bored with her new-found freedom. She decided to take up her husband's business where he had left off.

'He used to buy tumbledown hotels and do them up and sell them at vast profit!' she said, laughing at Dick's surprised face. 'Very profitable it was, and easy to make money if one has the capital to play with.'

'And this is what you have decided to do?'

She shook her head, her eyes teasing.

'No! I am actually doing it. Only my hotel is not like the ones my husband used to buy and sell. It is on a much bigger, grander scale. It is to be a kind of country club for the élite – very, very modern and very, very expensive. I open it next week. Why don't you come to the opening Gala night?'

Dick laughed.

'I'd love to but I don't live down here. I live in London.'

'It is not so far to come – twenty-five miles. I can promise you a very exciting evening.'

'I don't doubt it!' Dick said. 'But I do doubt if my wife would approve of the invitation.'

'So you have a wife – then bring her, too.

Would it interest you to hear about my venture?'

'Very much!' Dick said truthfully. 'But only on condition you dine with me. I suppose we can eat here?'

'That fits in with my plans very well!' she told him. 'I had planned to eat here because I've been told there is an exceptionally good chef. If it proves to be true, then I will buy him for my club. I have so far failed to acquire a good chef and that is absolutely essential for my kind of client.'

'Buy him?'

'Of course. Every man has his price. I will offer double what he gets here and he will come to me. It is as simple as that.'

'Sounds a trifle unscrupulous!' Dick laughed. 'However, by all means let's go and try him out.'

Over the meal, which was excellent, they exchanged more confidences. Dick discovered that his companion had no intention of running her hotel herself. As soon as it was well established, she would sell up and begin again somewhere else.

'It will take me just over a year and I expect to make at least thirty thousand pounds out of the deal!'

Dick whistled. Thirty thousand pounds was a very pleasant salary for a year's work. Provided one had the know-how, it would be fun buying up a stately home and

159

converting it, furnishing and staffing it. Staffing was probably the worst problem but this woman seemed to have managed to get all the labour she wanted. She told him she had imported Italians and Portuguese and had built flats for them to live in.

'With enough money, one can buy anything!' she said shrewdly.

Dick sighed. This talk of money reminded him of the sorry state of his own finances. This dinner was costing him at least six pounds he ought not to be spending. Tamily would be upset if she knew, but then it was Tam's fault he was here. If he had his way, he would have been dining with her, not with the Countess Helga von Routenhahn.

He looked across the table at his guest, frowning.

'You said your husband came from the North country. Is the name you use now your maiden name?'

She gave a low, husky laugh.

'No! It's a made-up name. I call myself that because it opens a lot of doors to me which my real name would not.'

Dick laughed outright, liking this strange woman.

'Well, that's honest enough. What is your real name.'

'Muriel Pratt. And my real accent, by the way, is pure Birmingham. That's where I was born.'

Dick found himself admiring her as well as enjoying her company. She had come a long way from being a shop assistant at seventeen. She'd married her husband for his money but she had been fond of him, too, and had helped him a great deal to make his first million.

'Of course, death duties took a huge whack of that,' she told Dick, 'but there's enough left for me to play around with and I intend to build it up to a million again. Money means power and I want power. I always did.'

'I want money, too!' Dick said. 'But not for the same reasons. I want to farm.'

She listened as he told her about his home. Dick intrigued her. She thought he was enormously attractive and had been momentarily disappointed to discover he was married. But marriage, she knew from past experience, was not necessarily a bar to an affair. It was not until Dick began to tell her more about Tamily that she realised this time a wife in the background could be a stumbling block, if this chance meeting was to lead to anything more.

Muriel Pratt sighed. Life was like that. For the first time in years she'd forgotten money and had begun to think first about sex. Trust her to pick on a man unlikely to be interested. All the same, he had asked her to dinner; was amused by her; possibly a little attracted to her despite the difference in their ages and despite the wife. There might be a chance…

'Why not come and have a look at my hotel?' she said casually. 'It's only twenty minutes' drive from here. It's empty, of course, but it might amuse you to look around. Do come if you've nothing better to do.'

Dick hesitated. It was too late now to drive back to London, pack a suitcase and go on down to Lower Beeches. He'd have to spend the night in Town and go down early next morning. There was really no reason why he couldn't go and see this fabulous country club. It would be better than the flat on his own for the remainder of the evening.

'The bar's stocked. We can help ourselves!' she said persuasively. 'What about it?'

'Okay, I'd love to!' Dick replied, beckoning to the waiter to bring him his bill.

Apparently the 'Countess' had no intention of buying the chef that evening – this would be done more subtly and less obtrusively tomorrow when he went off duty. She pointed out her car – a Triumph 2000, which made Dick draw in his breath with envy. He and Tamily ran a Vauxhall Estate van to make the carriage of prams and cots and cases easier between their two homes. But his real taste lay in sports cars.

'I'll lead the way!' she said, climbing into

162

her car and managing to show a great deal of slim nyloned leg in the process. Dick felt a momentary thrill of excitement, realising it was for his benefit.

But driving along behind her, he began to regret his impulse to go with her. It was all rather pointless since he would not see her again. If he'd been single – if there'd been no Tammy safe and secure in his heart – he might have enjoyed this adventure. But there wasn't going to be any repetition of Carol and no matter whether he found the 'Countess' attractive or not, he was not going to do anything he'd regret tomorrow.

By the time they turned in at the huge wrought iron gates of Colwyn's Country Club, Dick was once more wishing himself down at the farmhouse. Adam had probably stayed to supper to keep Tam company and although Sandra would be around for a while, she nearly always left when they'd washed up. Tammy and Adam would be alone and, however crazy the idea, he was filled with jealousy at the thought. Tammy would probably pour out her troubles into Adam's sympathetic ear and the pair of them would tell each other what a rotten husband and father he was.

Dick gave himself a shake. He was being unfair. Nobody could be more loyal than Tam; and Adam was as straight as a die. All the same, he wished he were there…

Then he saw the club. It had been a Tudor manor house; oak beams set in mellow brick and old red tiles on the roof. Someone had cleverly added a wing, joining the main building to what were once stables and, on the far side of the house, a further addition had been made, joining the house to a huge brick and timber barn. The result was very attractive and he whistled approvingly. A near-full moon made the place clearly visible and rather mysterious.

The Countess, as Dick now called her, climbed out of her car. She came over to stand beside him.

'Like it?' she asked. 'It'll be a lot more welcoming when the lights are on!'

She went into the building ahead of him, turning on switches and flooding the place with a soft warm glow. Everywhere, the décor and furniture had been chosen with the best of taste. The place looked like any wealthy man's home except for the more public rooms such as the dining-room and bar.

The Countess stopped at the bar and unlocking one of the cupboards below, poured out two brandies. She lifted her glass towards Dick and said softly:

'Welcome to my first guest!'

'It really is extremely nice!' Dick said approvingly. 'Here's to a big success for you.' They touched glasses. 'I admire your taste.'

The Countess laughed.

'It isn't really mine, although I very much approve. I employed an architect to replan the house and put on the extra wings and I had an interior decorator down from London to plan the décor. My husband used to say it always paid in the long run to buy the best advice.'

Dick leant on the bar, staring round him.

'I wonder if you will get the kind of people down here, willing to fork out what I imagine you will have to charge to make all this pay,' he said.

'I've no doubt about it. That, too, is really only a matter of money. Clever advertising and the right kick-off. That's why I've planned this Gala opening night. I've quite a few contacts among the London "smart young set", and I've sent out free invitations. If I can get them here once, I know they'll come back, with their friends. Come and see the barn where there'll be dancing. Then we'll go and see the pool.'

The barn had been transformed into a night club which Dick felt sure would appeal to the younger set. But the swimming pool was the biggest attraction. It was really a part of a huge natural lake. The gardens ran down in sloping lawns to this lake, the nearest part of which had been cleverly reconstructed to make the unusual grotto-like pool. His companion had

165

switched on floodlights concealed in the trees on either side and the water shone suddenly a deep translucent blue. Where the lawns came down to the water, a patio had been built on which stood tables and chairs where the bathers could sit and drink. There was also space enough to dance there on hot evenings.

Dick whistled approvingly again.

'I congratulate you – it's fabulous!' he said.

'Like a swim now?' she asked, looking up at him sideways from those curious slanting green eyes.

Dick laughed.

'I will if you will!'

But Muriel declined. She was too old to look her best with her hair dripping wet – only the very young could be completely natural and get away with it, she reminded herself. She was conscious, too, of her figure. That, too, did not show up to its best advantage undressed.

They sat down at one of the tables and smoked. The night air was heavy with summer scents and not at all cold. Dick looked beyond the swimming pool across the lake, shimmering in the moonlight.

Following his gaze, the Countess said.

'There are trout in the lake. Anyone who wants will be able to fish.'

Dick looked thoughtful.

'You know, I think something could be done about the lake. Not many people who come here will care a damn about fishing. But suppose there was water ski-ing! That's the newest sport and you've already got the biggest part of it – the water. You'd only need a take-off jetty built and a couple of speed boats, and there you are.'

'And a club house and boat house! What a magnificent idea, Dick. It could be done, I'm sure it could. I can't think how the idea never occurred to me.'

She looked at Dick, her excitement matching his own.

'If I'd only had you here a few months ago. Just think how well it would have gone down on my opening night – a flood-lit water ski-ing exhibition.'

Dick laughed.

'I don't see why you couldn't still do it. The boats could be bought easily enough and the water skis; you've already got electricity wired down here – it would only want extending. As to a boat house, you could probably get one of those ready-made prefabricated chalet hut things which would do, anyway temporarily. You could get a decent boat house and club house built later.'

Muriel Pratt remained silent. It was perfectly true – it *could* be done. It might even be the kind of gimmick which would make the place. Water ski-ing was popular ever since the Royals had taken it up and the lake was the perfect place for it. Running costs wouldn't be high. It was possible. But there was another reason which was prompting her to take Dick's idea seriously – Dick, himself. With every minute she spent in his company, she was becoming a little more attracted by him.

It was a very long while since she had met anyone like Dick, gay, amusing, sophisticated and yet somehow quite unspoilt. She was tired of the blasé rich young men she met in London; tired of the over-indulged wealthy business men who had tried to tempt her into a second marriage. The young men had been interested in her money; the old ones in her body. None had the fresh boyish innocence of Dick's that contrasted so excitingly with his self-assurance and experienced way with women. With his exceptional good looks, she did not doubt that he had always been chased by women. He was attractive but his main asset was a charm which was quite un-studied, as natural a part of him as his quick smile and ready enthusiasm for anything new. There was an aura of controlled energy about him, too, that was essentially youthful. He was young but he lacked the callow awkwardness of youth.

She knew she wanted this man; knew that it was not going to be easy to achieve her aim. Apart from their age difference, he had a young wife with whom he was obviously very much in love. But she was old enough and cynical enough to know that wives were not always stumbling blocks, even when their husbands loved them. Men were polygamous by nature and given the right time and place and opportunity, one could never guarantee they would be faithful.

'Let's go back to the bar,' she said thoughtfully. 'I could do with another drink while I think this out.'

Over the drinks, she began to question Dick about his home life, his job. It was not difficult for her to elicit that he was in some financial difficulty – a bad gamble on the stock market; that he had an urgent need to make big money quickly; that there was a difference of opinion with his wife about their young child. She was beginning at last to see a way to gain her own ends. Intelligent and shrewd, she knew that her approach must be subtle if it were ever to succeed.

'If you're not doing anything tomorrow, would you think it a mad proposition on my part to ask you to meet me here and work out this water ski-ing idea of yours? I think you've got something that could be enormously advantageous to this place. But I don't know the first thing about the sport myself and I would be tremendously grateful if you'd spare me an hour or two.'

Dick was flattered. The novelty of the whole situation struck him as highly bizarre. He was intrigued with the way Muriel Pratt was coping alone with this business venture. It struck him as a very solid one, and somehow he didn't doubt that she would make her million. But it took nerve and guts and it was unusual to find those qualities in a woman as attractive as his companion. She looked as if shc belonged on the cover of a glossy magazine or on the beach at St Tropez. One certainly did not meet her kind very often.

He'd like to come along tomorrow, but it would put paid to his plan to join Tamily at Lower Beeches. He wanted very much to go down and surprise her. He knew she would be miserable at the way he had behaved.

'I really ought to go down to my farm,' he said hesitantly. 'My wife–'

'Surely your wife would understand?' she broke in. 'After all, this is business, not pleasure.'

'Business?'

'Well, of course. I wouldn't expect to milk you of your ideas without first agreeing it was on a business basis.'

'What nonsense? My ideas, such as they are, are yours for the taking. You're more than welcome!'

'My husband would turn in his grave if he

heard you make that remark!' she said. 'He always said it was ideas which made money; that you should never give an idea away. It doesn't pay in this life to be generous, my dear friend.'

Dick laughed again.

'I daresay he was right, but I've no head for business. I suppose if I had, I wouldn't be sitting here worrying about my losses on the stock exchange – I'd be counting my millions in the bank.'

Muriel Pratt leant back in her chair and looked at him lazily through a cloud of smoke from her cigarette.

'Life is tough,' she commented, 'and you have to be tough to succeed. It's probably easier for people like me and my husband because we started with nothing and we learned early that we'd be stuck with nothing if we didn't toughen up. Now you began life with everything – you were never up against it, were you? Even now, you know you have your father behind you. You haven't the same incentive to succeed.'

'I've an incentive all right!' Dick said wryly. 'I admit it isn't the same incentive as yours but it's there all the same. Don't you think I'd give my right arm to make some money? I do have a certain amount of pride and it would just about finish me if I had to go back to my father with empty hands; not to mention the fact that I want to prove myself to my wife. Of course I'd make some money if I knew how!'

'Well, then, here's an opportunity. I've got a hell of a lot of capital tied up in this place. It really doesn't suit me right now to put in any more. Can you raise any capital?'

Not realising just how serious she was, Dick smiled and said:

'Well, I suppose if I sold out my shares at a loss, I could raise a few thousand but I can't see that being much good–' He broke off, leaning forward to stare at his companion. 'You mean to get this water ski-ing idea started?'

She nodded.

'Why not? It *is* a good idea. This place is only a stone's throw from London. People would come down at weekends, summer evenings. Those who came to ski would stay for meals and drinks. Oh, yes, indeed, it could provide the finishing touch. You finance it and you can take a fair share of the profits. I've made it a limited company for tax purposes and I'll offer you a fair proportion of shares.'

Dick drew in his breath.

'Well, I must say it's tempting. You say you're going to sell out the whole caboosh in a year – that means we'd realise our capital then, plus profits. Of course, it is a gamble...'

'But it could easily make back for you what you'll lose on those dud shares you are holding now and plus. Well, think it over, Dick. I'll meet you back here tomorrow about eleven-thirty. You can tell me then what you've decided.'

'You really mean this?'

'I'm completely in earnest. You've offered me a splendid opportunity to expand my present outlay. If you'd like to come in on a partnership basis, I'd be more than pleased to have you. It's up to you now to decide if you want to join in with me.'

Dick finished his brandy at a gulp. It was, of course, a crazy idea and yet it made sense. He stared round the empty room and imagined how it might be in a few weeks' time, crammed with people talking, laughing, drinking. It wasn't hard to imagine; not so hard as to believe that this was not some dream and that he would wake up and find there was no such person as the 'Countess'; no such place as the club; no such possibility as the lake shimmering out there in the moonlight.

He felt excitement rising in him. Maybe this was one of those queer strokes of Fate; a moment in time which could change his whole life or certainly make a change in his fortunes. But for his impulsive whim to go to Brighton to watch a cricket match, his equally impulsive decision to go back to London, he would never have known this place existed. He felt almost as if the whole day had been prearranged, had been meant to happen.

'Oh, Tam!' he thought. 'Maybe this is the one chance we need to get us back to Lower Beeches for good!'

Surely anything was worth a try which could achieve this. Years of hard work as a stockbroker had ended with them being no nearer that goal. Now maybe in a few months he could get back on his feet; recoup his losses and show Tam that he was worth something after all.

Watching his face, reading his expression, Muriel Pratt relaxed. She had little doubt what his decision would be.

TWELVE

On Sunday night, Dick returned to the flat jubilant. He could not wait to tell Tamily about his new project. But Tamily was not waiting for him at the flat although it was long past Richard's bedtime and normally they would have been back from the country at least a couple of hours earlier.

He had driven back to London feeling on top of the world. During the day, he and Muriel had thrashed out the plans in detail for the water-ski club and tomorrow Muriel was meeting him at her solicitor's office in London to make their partnership legal. Dick was to sell his shares for whatever he could get and reinvest the money in what seemed to him a foolproof money-winner. Only now in the silent rooms did he remember that he and Tamily had parted for the weekend on anything but good terms; that it was vitally important he put his personal as well as his financial affairs in order.

He telephoned home. Tamily answered.

'Oh, so you're back!' Her voice was cool and distinctly unfriendly.

'Darling, don't be that way! I've some

wonderful news for you. But first tell me why you're still down there? Nothing wrong, is there?'

There was a slight pause. Then she said:

'On the contrary, we're all fine. Richard's been doing so well, wearing his aid. I decided the country suits him better than London. I shan't come back until Wednesday. I have to be back for Thursday because the teacher is coming.'

'But, Tam, I can't possibly come down and join you, you know that. Besides, I've a particularly important engagement tomorrow which you won't want me to break when you hear about it—'

'I'm not suggesting you come down,' Tamily broke in. 'You can manage for a day or two on your own up there, can't you?'

Dick drew in his breath sharply. Things were worse than he had thought. Obviously Tamily was determined to make him realise just how upset she was.

'Of course I can manage!' he said reasonably. 'But I would like you here, Tam. I've so much to tell you and talk over with you. It's urgent, too. Surely you could come back tomorrow?'

'I could but I don't want to, for Richard's sake,' Tamily replied flatly.

'What do you mean, for Richard's sake!'

'Well, if you want to know, he's willing to wear his aid when Adam puts it on. Adam makes a game of it and Richard thinks it's fun.'

'Can't *you* make a game of it?' Dick said. 'What's so special about Adam?'

'Only that he's tremendously patient and has the right way with Richard.'

'Meaning I haven't!'

There was silence on the line connecting them. Dick was furiously jealous. Moreover, he was unhappily aware that he wasn't prepared to get on his hands and knees and fiddle around with that confounded deaf contraption.

'If Adam's so all-fired wonderful, it's a pity you aren't married to him instead of me.'

'Don't be childish, Dick!'

'And don't you talk to me as if I were two years old. I have some rights as your husband and I want you back here, do you understand?'

'I understand what you want, Dick, but I'm sorry, this time I'm not prepared to sacrifice Richard just because you've some crazy scheme in mind.'

'And how do you know it's crazy when you don't even know what it's all about? You won't even let me tell you about it.'

'And you won't even let me tell you about the help Richard needs from you, so that makes us even. I'll be back on Wednesday, Dick. Good night!'

He could not believe that she had rung

off. White-hot anger gave way to an acute depression. Everything had seemed to be going so splendidly all day and now this. The contrast was almost too much to put up with. Trust a wife to be the damper to his good spirit. Muriel certainly understood and shared his enthusiasm. In fact hers outmatched his own.

He put on his jacket and went out to a nearby Italian restaurant for a meal. After he had eaten and drunk a half bottle of white wine, he felt a little better. By Wednesday Tam would be in a different mood. When she came back, he'd have this new business scheme all tied up and she'd be as thrilled as he was about it. It wasn't good for husbands and wives to be too much together. A day or two apart once in a while was good for marriage. He'd read that in a book. Tamily would begin to miss him. A nice welcome and no recriminations from him and all would be well.

In fact, the more he thought about it, the better the idea seemed that she should be away just now. He'd be pretty tied up these next few days and he'd be free to run down to the club with Muriel in the evenings if Tam weren't at home waiting for him. He would take Muriel out to dinner. That would be a tactical move and fun, too. Not that he had any intention of letting their partnership become more than platonic.

One woman in his life was quite enough to cope with!

At Lower Beeches, Tamily put down the receiver and turned to Adam with eyes that were brimming with tears.

'He doesn't care in the least about Richard!' she burst out. 'All he can think about is himself. If he really cared, he'd be down here to fetch us. I'd half expected him all day.'

Adam got up and poured her a drink.

'Steady up!' he said soothingly. 'You weren't exactly encouraging him to come, you know. I'd say your remarks as well as your tone were distinctly unfriendly!'

Tamily sniffed and then smiled.

'Oh, I suppose you're right, though I hate you for saying it. But I was cross... I am cross with him, Adam. He just won't take life seriously.'

Adam lit his pipe with slow deliberation. Then he said:

'I think Dick is taking life much more seriously now than at one time. No one, least of all your father-in-law, believed Dick would knuckle down to a nine-to-five job. It can't have been easy for him with his volatile temperament. I think he must love you very much in his own way, Tamily, to have stuck it out so long.'

Tamily sighed.

'You're very loyal to him, aren't you,

Adam? I suppose I ought not to be talking about him like this to you, but you know Dick as well as I do, and you being so fond of him makes a difference.'

'Sometimes I wish that I didn't like him quite so much!' Adam said, and quickly smiled to cover the lapse. 'Seriously, Tamily, since you have brought up the subject, let me give you a word of advice. Don't let Richard become a bone of contention between you and Dick. I know Richard does need you both, but you can't force people to feel as you do. Dick will come around to it if you can only give him time.'

For the first time in her life, Tamily turned away from him.

'Richard hasn't got time to be wasted!' she said, her voice suddenly hard. 'I'm sorry, Adam, but this is one occasion when Dick's going to have to do things my way.'

'And if he won't?'

'Then I'll carry on by myself. I'll come and live down here where I can give all my time to Richard. I've Mother and Dick's parents and Sandra and *you*, Adam. You'll all help me with him, I know.'

Adam said nothing. He was deeply concerned now at Tamily's state of mind. In this he could not agree with her entirely. A family was a unit and all the members should be considered equally. It must be wrong for a mother to concentrate so much on her child, even a handicapped child, that her relationship with her husband suffered. If Dick became jealous of Richard, his attitude to the child would be even more in jeopardy. But Tamily seemed not to care. Maybe because she knew that if Dick wouldn't help, he, Richard's godfather, would. And that made their friendship wrong for the first time. It was right that Tamily could depend upon his friendship but never upon him as a replacement father for Dick's child.

A feeling of utter dejection came over Adam. His heart had always told him what was right and what was wrong. He'd known for years that his love for Tamily was only permissible provided he never let it encroach upon her marriage. Once before Tamily had turned to him on the rebound when Dick had failed her. It was not unlikely that she would do the same now, knowing, as she must, that he loved her; knowing that he loved the children, Richard in particular. The situation was no longer innocent. So it ought to end.

Unable to bear his train of thought, Adam excused himself on the grounds of tiredness and left the house. The garden was bathed in moonlight, a golden light for this was a harvest moon. The big copper beech trees cast a great dark shadow over the lawn. Beneath them, he caught a glimpse of something pale, white, moving.

'Is someone there?' he called out.

The figure came out from the shadows and approached him. It was Sandra, her white cotton frock startling in the velvety night. Her feet were bare.

'I was just walking!' she said softly. 'It was too hot to sleep!'

She turned her face up to his as she spoke and he saw the softly rounded cheek, the lashes full and dark outlining her eyes.

Life was cruel! he thought suddenly. Nature was cruel. It trapped human beings by their emotions. This girl was not Tamily, but she was young and appealing and invitingly beautiful. He could not love her but he could and did desire her.

She said nothing, but stood there, her bare arms hanging loosely at her sides, her face upturned, tilted a little as if in question.

'I'll walk home with you,' Adam said.

She gave a soft laugh.

'I'm not going home. I'm sleeping here tonight. But I'll walk home with you, shall I?'

'All right!' The words seemed to be dragged from him. The night was so soft, so inviting. Not a night to be alone.

He felt her warm hand slip into his and they began to walk. Her bare feet kicked up the dew on the grass so that they appeared to be phosporescent. She was no longer Sandra but a night nymph, a magical goddess come from the woods to tempt him.

They left the lawn and turned into the wood. There the moonlight lay in dappled patches on the path. Sometimes it flashed on her silky hair, sometimes it illuminated their joined hands. All around them, there were the movements of nocturnal wood creatures. Adam could identify most of them but he was oblivious to everything but the girl's soft breathing. Once or twice she looked up at him smiling but she said nothing. Part of her enchantment lay in her silence.

In the very heart of the wood, he stopped and, without warning, caught her up in his arms. His mouth came down on hers brutally, without tenderness, hungry and demanding.

She returned his kisses passionately. Her mouth, her body encouraging and not rejecting him. They fell on to the grass and he pulled her close to him again so that she lay along the length of his body. He kissed her again, his mouth bruising her soft lips.

Once, he cried out harshly:

'You are so beautiful. It's not right.'

She silenced him with her lips.

They were both trembling violently now, caught up in a mutual passionate need. In the last moments of sanity, Adam cried out:

'This is wrong, Sandra. I'm in love with *her.*'

'I know, I know, but I love you!' she whispered. 'I love you, Adam. I want you to take me.'

A moment earlier, he might have done so, quickly and cruelly. Now, suddenly, he knew that it could not be this way. Sandra was innocent and the first time must be with a man who loved her, who would marry her. He could do neither.

She lay against him, her white dress torn from one rounded shoulder, the curve of her breast exposed above his hand. She was all woman, warm, fragrant, enticing and utterly surrendered to his desire, yet he could not take his advantage over her. Sandra was no farm girl out for a tumble in the hay. She was young and innocent and she loved and trusted him.

She put a hand tentatively against his cheek.

'What's wrong? Don't you want me?' she asked.

'Oh, God, yes! But not this way, Sandra. That would be wrong.'

She flung her arms round him, pressing herself against him. Her eyes shone with tears.

'It cannot be wrong – I love you!' she cried. 'I'll never love anyone else. Give me this one night, Adam – just this one night. I know you don't love me. I don't ask for your love – only that you'll let me belong to you just this one night.'

'Do you know what you are saying?' His voice sounded harsh as the words were torn from him. She must know that he was not made of stone; that his life had been far too long without the solace of a woman. She was near enough to nature to know how easy it was to tempt a man, weaken him into losing all sense of right and wrong. She must be aware that she was playing with fire.

'Yes, I know!' Her voice was clear and certain. 'I know that I love you. I know that something sent you out of that house away from *her* to me. I knew all evening that you would come. I waited for you. It is not for you I ask but for myself. Take me, Adam. Please!'

A cloud drifted lazily across the moon. It was no longer possible for them to see each other. He felt her hands reach beneath his jacket, undo the buttons of his shirt and then lie warm and throbbing against his chest. In the darkness an owl hooted, calling to its mate. His arms reached out of their own volition, drawing her closer and closer to him. She was a woman of the moonlight, a myth, offering him solace and forgetfulness and body's ease.

The urgency was suddenly gone and in its place was tenderness. Gently, his strong brown hands against her fair skin, he helped her to take off the white dress.

185

'We must get married!'

His voice was low and husky. She sat up and began to straighten her clothes and hair. He lay on his back, watching her, waiting for her reply. She did not look at him as she said:

'No, Adam. I won't marry you.'

'But, Sandra…' he propped himself up on one elbow and reached out to touch her hair gently with his hand. 'Of course we must be married now.'

She turned and reached for his hand, pulling it down from her head to her cheek which she rested against it.

'There is no "of course"! There were no obligations. What happened just now was not your fault.'

Adam withdrew his hand.

'It was as much my fault as yours,' he said. 'I am older enough to have more control.'

Suddenly, he saw tears glistening on her cheeks and very tenderly he wiped them away. Misunderstanding their cause, he said:

'You're not to worry, Sandra. Everything will be all right. We shall get married as soon as possible. That's a promise.'

'You don't understand, do you?' she cried out. 'I don't *want* to marry you. Do you think I could bear to live with the thought that you'd married me out of a sense of obligation? Duty? I love you, Adam. Unless you loved me, too, I couldn't bear to share my life with you.'

He remained silent, knowing that he could not tell her what she needed to know. He did not love her. His heart was in Tamily's keeping. He wasn't free to love her. Yet, in a way, he did feel some very special affection for her. It surprised him that their moments of love-making had been so beautiful, so complete, so right. Were it not for Tamily—

'I'm going back to the house!' Sandra said quietly. 'Don't come with me... I want to go alone. And Adam...' She was standing up now, looking down at him, her face in shadow so that he could not read her expression. 'Adam, in the morning when you wake up, forget this ever happened. We shall be certain to run into each other ... it will be easier for both of us if we go on as if this night had never existed.'

He jumped to his feet and went to put his arms around her. He felt confused and guilty and helpless. Her cool pride and control evoked his admiration and yet strangely, it hurt, too. He knew he would be unable to forget their love-making and, selfish though it might be, he hated to think that she could behave as if nothing at all had happened between them.

For a moment, she softened in his arms, her body curved and clinging, warm and once more inviting. But as he bent his head to kiss her, she suddenly pulled herself out of his embrace and began to run away from him, into the dark shadows beneath the trees lining the path. He took a step forward as if to go after her but then his arms fell to his sides and he remained standing alone. He knew that his own home awaited him, empty, without warmth or companionship. He had no desire to return to it. Just for this little while, he had known close companionship with another human being; he had known the comfort and unbelievable beauty of lying with a woman who loved him. What they had shared had indeed been beautiful for in the ultimate moment he had forgotten even Tamily and Sandra had been his world. He wanted to go back to that forgetfulness of self; to the feeling of being part of another; of sharing. He was tired of being alone.

He began to walk slowly towards his house. The moonlight was as brilliant and mystical as ever. He could not stop his thoughts. He wondered if he would feel differently in the morning when this strange night was done and the sun came up bright and golden. Perhaps then, this would seem like a dream and he would be able to forget, as Sandra suggested, that they had ever made love. He knew that he ought to feel more guilt. However much she might try to take the blame for what had happened, his was the ultimate responsibility for he was older, in years anyway. He knew that he was responsible and wished desperately that she had agreed to marry him. Such a marriage might work. Maybe Sandra could help him to put Tamily out of his heart. Certainly she had the power to assuage all physical desire.

But what could *he* give *Sandra?* A home of her own, a secure financial position. He was well paid by Lord Allenton and he never spent money since he had nothing to spend it on. He had enough saved to be able to buy and set up his own farm though he had never once contemplated doing so; the thought of leaving the Allentons after all these years was out of the question. But if Sandra could be persuaded to marry him, she could do up the house the way she wanted it, without any money worries. They could afford a family...

Suddenly, the colour rushed into Adam's face and he caught his breath. There could be a child resulting from tonight. Sandra had not considered it and nor had he until this moment. In a strange way, the idea held a deep thrill and excitement for him. He loved children ... had nursed a secret desire for his own for years. It was no longer just a dream but a real possibility that his son might actually be born in the Spring of next year. It would be the first Spring when the sight of all the young lambs and calves, kittens and piglets, chickens, puppies and pheasant chicks did not fill him with envy as well as joy. He, alone, was without a new young life. Now, perhaps...

Without knowing it, Adam had arrived at his front door. He pushed it open and walked inside, his head held high, his eyes bright and filled with hope and determination. In the morning, he would seek out Sandra; make her see that marriage was the only right solution. If she truly loved him, as she had said, he could surely over-persuade her. If he could not offer her the ultimate peak of love, he could offer her at least a very deep and sincere affection. He would do everything in his power to make her happy. He would care for her with all the tenderness of which he knew himself capable. He had not realised it until now but he really needed her.

Slowly, thoughtfully, he undressed and went to bed. It was a long time before he could sleep. He knew that what had happened was real and yet already it had the unreality of a remembered dream. He could not understand why Sandra should love him. Even harder to understand why she had decided to throw away her innocence, turning her back on girlhood, just for one brief moment of pleasure. It was out of keeping with her character which he knew to be steady, deep-thinking, intelligent. But then, he reminded himself, love could make people behave in ways that were normally foreign to them. It could raise them to great heights and reduce them to the lowest depths of despair. None should know that better than he. But he would not wish despair on Sandra, sweet, lovely Sandra. He must make absolutely sure in the morning that she was not the one ultimately to suffer because of his hungry need of her and the children she could give him.

When finally he slept, it was to dream that he held her once more in his arms. But this time she withheld herself from him – always just beyond his reach, tantalising and tempting him but never assuaging his desire.

'No, Adam,' she said. 'You love Tamily and you cannot have us both.'

THIRTEEN

Dick meant to be home in time to welcome Tamily and Richard on Wednesday but a telephone call from Muriel changed his plans at the last moment. The country club was opening on the Saturday and there was a mass of things to be seen to before then.

'I really need you down at the club as soon as you leave the office,' she said. 'I wouldn't ask you if it wasn't important, Dick. I know this is the evening you are expecting your wife back. But you can explain to her later, can't you?'

Dick's part-ownership was now tied up legally and he was well aware that he could not possibly let Muriel down now after all her extraordinary kindness to him in letting him in on the project. Of course Tam would understand, he told himself. He ordered a large bunch of carnations to be delivered in the late afternoon with a note from him attached saying, *Welcome home, darling. See you about nine p.m. Will explain everything then.*

But he had misjudged Tamily's mood. Knowing nothing of his new partnership, she could think of no valid reason why he could not have come home from work at the usual time. Even Dick, she told herself, was not so insensitive that he was unaware of the rift between them. She had thought that by remaining on at Lower Beeches after the weekend, she would show him clearly that she was upset and angry at his attitude to Richard. She wasn't going to permit him to ignore their quarrel and put it right with a bunch of flowers.

But as the evening wore on, and still Dick did not appear, she began to wonder where he could be. If he were taking a client out to drinks, which sometimes he did, he usually managed to get away by nine. It was now past ten. She was tired and ready for bed but stubbornly refused to go until Dick was home. Her resentment against him mounted.

When at eleven-thirty he finally opened the front door and called out to her, she was so tensed she could not trust her voice to form a normally casual reply. Dick came into the sitting-room. She could see at once that he was in good spirits – that far from looking worried or anxious, he was on top of the world.

'You're still up then, darling? How lovely to have you back. I've missed you desperately. How are you, darling?'

He came towards her but she turned her head sideways, avoiding his kiss.

'Oh, hell, Tam, don't be like that. I *had* to

193

be late. Look, darling, let me explain and then you'll see why I wasn't here to greet you this evening.'

He went over to the drinks cupboard and poured himself a drink. Knowing him so well, she could feel his excitement and her heart sank. Dick was obviously in the throes of some new idea that was absorbing him completely. Even now he wasn't really thinking about her – or Richard.

He began to tell her about his extraordinary meeting with Muriel Pratt. Tamily listened with growing unease. It had not occurred to her that Dick's excitement could be due to another woman. She'd trusted him completely since Carol and now she suddenly saw that she had been crazy to believe Dick could change. He would never be proof against a clever, pretty woman's wiles.

'I'm not particularly anxious to hear about the other women in your life,' she began, but Dick broke in, laughing.

'Don't be such a goof, Tam. This is a *business* partnership. If you'll just let me finish you'll understand.'

He continued his story – describing the club and the lake and how he had sold his shares and now had a stake in Muriel Pratt's investment.

'Don't you see, darling, by this time next year, we'll have made back everything I've lost. And Muriel gave me the chance. Of course I couldn't back out this evening. The boats were being delivered and I had to be there.'

Tamily felt a cold shiver run down her spine. This was the same irresponsible madcap boy of the past. He'd learned nothing in these years of marriage – nothing at all. He'd been willing to gamble all their savings once on the stock exchange and as if that were not sufficient warning, had now done the same thing again, giving some completely strange woman all his capital for her mad venture.

'I think you're absolutely crazy!' she said coldly. 'I think it is far more likely that by this time next year you will have lost everything we had left, and at a time when we need money more than ever. Have you forgotten Richard? Can't you ever think of me?'

Dick stared at her wide-eyed.

'But, Tam, that's just exactly why I've done this – for you and the boy. This time next year I can probably afford to take him over to America where I'm absolutely sure a cure can be found for him. It is for you both!'

He sounded so hurt and indignant that for a split second she nearly wavered. But she steeled herself against what she felt to be weakness and said:

'I suppose it's too late to back out so there's no point in our discussing what you've done. All I can say is that I want no part in it. As to you taking Richard to America I want no part in that either. The sooner you accept the fact that he's deaf and going to be deaf all his life, the better. He's begun to wear his aid and one day I'm going to have him talking just like other children, whether you like it or not.'

The bubble of excitement on which he had ridden home was now truly burst. Dick stared at Tamily silently. This was not the girl he knew and loved; not his sweet, understanding Tam. Her lack of faith in him hurt him bitterly and the contrast between her opinion of him and Muriel's was all too marked. If Tam didn't want him, Muriel had made it all too clear that she did. Of course, he'd pretended not to notice the advances Muriel made; the veiled suggestions; the gestures that showed she found him more than a little attractive. He wanted their association to remain completely platonic and he'd not given her one single reason to think otherwise. His parting words to Muriel had been that he was going to bring his wife down to the club as soon as it was open, for a second honeymoon. Some honeymoon it would be with Tam in this mood.

'I'm going to bed!' Tamily announced. Dick put out a hand to restrain her.

'You obviously want to provoke a quarrel,' he said, 'but I'm not going to let you. It's all so silly. I've acted in what I believe are our joint interests. I don't see why you should jump to the conclusion I'm wrong. It is a gamble, I suppose, but the rewards are more than worth the risk. I want money. Tam – money so that we can go and live at Lower Beeches. We've never been really happy living in Town – it doesn't suit either of us. As for Richard – well, I'm sorry I can't see things your way but I'd be wrong to pretend I did. I think it's better for him to be cured rather than treated. *Is* that so wrong?'

'Not wrong, but stupid, seeing that the specialists say there is no hope of an operation putting things right. You've got to accept the facts, Dick, whether you like them or not.'

Dick let go her arm. Depression now had its grip firmly on him. He said slowly:

'I just can't face the facts if the facts are that my son is going to have to wear that ruddy contraption strung round him all his life. I don't want to be hard on the kid but I know I couldn't feel the same way towards him if every time I looked at him I had to be reminded that he was abnormal. I'd pity him but I don't think I could feel the same pride in him. I'm sorry if that hurts you, Tam, but it's the truth.'

She stared at him, her eyes enormous and expressing both indignation and misery in equal parts.

'At least you're being honest now,' she said, the words dragging slowly from her lips. 'At least we now all know where we stand. One thing is clear, we can't go on living together. I'd begin to hate you every time you looked at Richard. Even now I find it hard to forgive you for denying him your support for something that isn't his fault. Perhaps it's fortunate that he isn't going to miss you as much as some boys might miss their fathers. He does, after all, have Adam who adores him. It was Adam who got him to wear his aid last weekend and Richard's accepted it now. Maybe it'll be better for all of us if I take him away from you. We can go and live at Lower Beeches. I can get a teacher of the deaf for him down there.'

'Are you off your head?' Dick shouted. 'Do you honestly mean to let a thing like this bust up our marriage? What about you and me? Don't we count? To listen to you, Richard is the only one of the three of us who has to be considered. We're a family, not one handicapped child. And like it or not, you're my wife, Tamily. I'm not going to be shoved on one side as if I didn't matter.'

'Still thinking only of yourself!' Tamily said bitingly. 'It has to be what you want, what you need, doesn't it? Well, I'm not concerned with you any more. I'm putting Richard's needs first whether you like it or not. At least he will have one parent whom he can depend on to love and help him.'

Dick was staring at her, his face flushed,

his blue eyes blazing angrily.

'I think you're out of your mind. Or maybe Adam Bond has put you up to this. Maybe you've come to the conclusion he'd make a better father for Richard than me?'

'Maybe I have. I think he would, too!'

'Then you can damn well go and find out for sure,' Dick shouted at her, beyond reason now. 'Maybe he won't turn out to be quite the golden boy you suspect. And don't expect me to sit twiddling my thumbs waiting for you to come back crying that you made a mistake, because I probably won't be here. There are other women in the world – women like Muriel who thinks I'm worth something. You've been despising me just a little too long, Tamily. I'm sick to death of it. Well, have your separation and see if I care.'

Desperately afraid that she might burst into humiliating tears, Tamily hurried out of the room. She had had no intention of quarrelling like this with Dick. How could it have happened that they were actually discussing a separation as if it were not only possible but desirable?

FOURTEEN

Dick, too, was regretting his lost temper but it never occurred to him that this particular quarrel was really the end of their marriage. He fully believed that by morning Tamily would have woken in a better frame of mind, eager to make it up; to listen to his explanations and plans and see for herself that he was only trying to do what he could for her and for the boy.

But Tamily refused to speak to him, cooking breakfast for him as always, talking to Richard as if he, Dick, did not exist. He began to feel thoroughly angry with her. Moreover, the sight of his son sitting at table wearing the deaf aid not only upset him but he felt that Tamily had put it on deliberately to aggravate him. After all, if the child really did have to wear it, surely he could do so when he, Dick, was not around to see. Tamily knew very well how he felt about seeing Richard wired up like a dummy – the least she could do was to use a little tact. It was almost as if she were challenging him to say something about it – but he wasn't going to. Two could play at her game. He stalked off to the office without even saying goodbye.

As the front door closed behind him, tears pricked at Tamily's eyes; tears she only just managed to control for Richard's sake. She could understand Dick going off in a temper without saying a word to her – but the studied way he avoided even looking at the little boy had hurt her desperately. She guessed it was partly due to the fact that she'd put on Richard's aid but then Dick had to get used to the sight of it just as Richard had had to get used to wearing it. If Dick really couldn't subjugate his feelings for his son's sake, then maybe it really would be best for them to separate. She wasn't going to allow anything in the world to stand between her and her plans to have Richard talking like any other child.

'Let Dick find out just how much he misses us!' she thought rebelliously. 'It'll do him good to be on his own!'

But even as she told herself this, she began to wonder. Who was this woman, Muriel something, Dick had met? Was it really just a business venture or was Dick up to his old tricks? Perhaps she had been unfair to accuse him without knowing all the facts, but then Dick had hardly inspired her trust in the past. It was his own fault if she thought the worst of him rather than the best. And even if it were all business as Dick swore it was, he'd no right to gamble with their money when Richard might need so many extras.

Something of her own inner tensions and conflicts must have communicated themselves to the boy. When the teacher came Richard, contrary to his usual placid nature, was tearful and completely unco-operative. Nothing was achieved and he finally refused to wear the aid at all. Nerves strung to breaking point, Tamily burst into tears. She had really had no intention of confiding in the grey-haired, middle-aged woman who had come to help her with Richard's training. But years of visiting parents with handicapped children had given the woman a thorough insight into the problems and tensions that grew in any household where the family life was inevitably disorganised by such a child. She was not in the least surprised to hear of Dick's reactions. She had met up before with fathers who couldn't face the fact that their child was in some way imperfect. There were others who were jealous because their wives gave too much time to the children; sometimes difficulties arose with other children in the family who might feel neglected, put aside, and therefore developed behaviour problems. Sometimes it was easier for the mothers who didn't care quite as much about their children – who weren't as intensely devoted as Tamily Allenton.

'You must remember, my dear, that you are a wife as well as a mother. Give your husband time – he'll get used to it.'

'No, he won't!' Tamily cried bitterly. 'You don't know him.'

She wouldn't, to a stranger, say: 'Dick's selfish – he always has been. He really only cares about himself.' But the thought was there and no matter how much this woman might talk to her about using a little tact and a lot of patience with Dick, she knew her mind was already made up. She'd go back to Lower Beeches with Richard. Adam would help her. She didn't really *need* Dick. If he really loved her – and Richard – he would come down after them. The choice would be his and the sooner she found out the truth, the better. If she did go back to him, it would be on her terms; terms that included complete acceptance of Richard's treatment and a clear understanding that *he* came first.

Tamily was unprepared for the reception she was to receive from her mother. For the first time in her life, Jess was clearly angry.

'You talk about Dick being selfish, Tamily, but what about you? Richard isn't just your son, you know. He belongs equally to Dick. As head of the family, it's really for him to have the last word, not you, although I agree it should be a joint decision.'

Tamily stared at her mother wide-eyed. She was too surprised to answer for a moment. Then she said:

'You really believe I'd sit back and let Richard remain deaf and dumb just to satisfy

Dick's selfish whims?'

'Don't be silly, Tamily,' Jess said sharply, hearing the hysteria behind Tamily's voice. 'You know as well as I do that Dick would soon realise for himself something must be done for the boy. He can't help his reactions any more than you can. You accuse him of not considering you or Richard in the matter, but tell me just how much you are considering him. It's been a terrible shock for him and of the two of you, I'd say Dick is probably feeling it more even than you. He idolised the boy – thought him perfect in every way. As his mother, you no doubt still see him as perfect but he isn't – he's handicapped and abnormal and Dick needs time to get used to the idea.'

Tamily caught her breath.

'Why?' she almost shouted. 'Adam hasn't turned against Richard. Adam can go on loving him and he isn't even his child.'

'Adam isn't Dick!' Jess said quietly. 'And he isn't your husband, Tamily. I wouldn't have spoken of this but I think it's time I did. You rely far too much on Adam and not enough on Dick. I'm not suggesting that your motives are anything but innocent – I know you're not in love with Adam or anything like that. But I'm sure you know as well as I do that Adam has been in love with you for years. And you've no right to trade on that love. If you really cared about him as a person, you'd see a lot less of him and give him the chance to get over the way he feels about you and start thinking of someone else. But for you, Adam might be married to Sandra and that, if you ask me, is the best possible thing that could happen to him. He wants children, sons of his own – not a half share in yours!'

Tamily was so shaken she was speechless. Deep in her heart she knew that every word Jess had spoken was the truth. But she was appalled and dismayed that Jess, for a long time, had seen this truth and never until now spoken her mind.

'I suppose you think I've been very selfish!' she whispered.

Jess' face softened.

'I don't think it was intentional, Tamily. You were very ill after Richard was born and Adam has such a kind, soothing, gentle nature – anyone would have welcomed a friend like that. But he's not so young, you know, that he can afford to go on wasting his youth. He should get married and I think Sandra is in love with him. Let him go, Tamily, and by that I mean, don't let him know that you need him – not even for Richard. Let him realise you can manage and be happy without him.'

'But I can't!' Tamily cried. 'I need him more than ever now. I need him to help me with Richard.'

Jess put a hand on Tamily's shoulder.

'You cannot have Adam as a substitute for Dick. If you really intend to live apart from Dick, then you must face up to the fact that you'll have to go it alone – alone, Tamily, or at least, only with my help. I'll do what I can.'

Tamily's eyes dropped from her mother's face. She knew with every core of her being that Jess was right. But was she strong enough to do as Jess suggested – manage without Adam? She wasn't sure.

'Suppose'... she began hesitantly and then with more strength, said, 'Suppose I decided to divorce Dick – marry Adam?'

'Then for the first time in my life, I'd find myself despising you and pitying you, Tamily. You married Dick for better or for worse, remember? I couldn't respect any woman who throws her husband over when she has to face a little of the "worse". Maybe it won't hurt the two of you to be separated for a while. But divorce so that you can marry Adam? No, Tamily, and in your heart you know I'm right. You aren't in the least in love with him. You just want the love he has to offer you and you've absolutely no right whatever to that, no matter what Dick has done.'

'Maybe I don't love Adam, but I don't love Dick any more either. He's finally killed my love. I don't care if I never see him again.'

'I know!' Jess said soothingly. What she

206

really meant was that she'd heard Tamily use those same words before but knew that, like all women, Tamily could not control the illogical demands of her heart.

FIFTEEN

Adam was deeply hurt. Since Tamily's return to Lower Beeches, he'd seldom been invited there for meals and the old, easy companionship they had shared had become strained and awkward when they did meet.

He wondered, guiltily, if she had somehow heard about Sandra. Only Sandra could have told her what had happened between them that night and it struck him as very improbable that she would talk of such a thing to Tamily. But he could see no other explanation for the sudden change in Tamily's behaviour.

It was true that she spent ninety per cent of her time with the boy. Richard was making wonderful progress, too. She seemed happy and contented about the child. Of her relationship with Dick she said little except that Dick hated the sight of Richard's deaf aid, and they'd mutually agreed to live apart for the time being so that their disagreement about the child's treatment did not erupt into a series of quarrels over the child which could adversely affect him.

It wasn't for Adam to criticise but he felt Dick ought to be there with her, taking care of her and doing his share for his son. At least he should come down for weekends. Tamily said he would have been down except that he was very much caught up in the new Country Club he now had shares in and which was newly opened and apparently doing very well. Dick had to go down there most weekends to keep an eye on the water ski-ing side of things which was the Club's main attraction.

Adam felt the more depressed because Sandra, too, ignored him. It was as if that night between them simply hadn't existed. He had tried desperately to get her to consider marrying him but she'd said for the second time: 'I don't want to marry you, Adam. I just want to forget that night ever happened.'

But he couldn't forget. The sweetness, the strange magical hour in the wood haunted his sleeping as well as his waking moments. He was afraid Sandra felt ashamed and he could not feel ashamed because it had all seemed so strangely right. She said she loved him and yet her behaviour now indicated the opposite for she avoided him whenever possible, and the occasional times they did meet on the estate or in church or at Lower Beeches, she looked hurriedly away as if she were anxious to avoid speaking to him. It both worried and upset him and when he wasn't thinking about Tamily, he was thinking about her, Sandra. If his relationship with Tamily had not been so strained, he might even have asked her advice about Sandra. But Tamily was as unapproachable as Sandra herself.

There was really only Jess to talk to. He was very fond of Jess and although they had never discussed anything intimately, he always felt her friendly liking for him and that she understood him. He wondered if Jess would be very shocked to know what had happened in the woods. Not that he could ever tell her or anyone else in the world for that matter. It was Sandra's secret and he could never talk about it – only think about it and marvel at how it had come about; how they could either of them have stepped so much out of character.

'She ought to marry me!' he told himself for the hundredth time. It was only right and proper that she should. Couldn't she see that he would do everything in the world to make her happy? Moreover, he needed her, not just as a woman, and his physical longing for her tormented him incessantly now – but as a companion. He was lonely – desperately lonely.

About a month after Tamily's return to Lower Beeches, Sandra's mother fell ill with a 'flu virus. Tamily said at once that she could spare Sandra to go and take over her mother's job looking after Adam for the few days she was laid up.

Sandra tried hard to find an excuse not to go.

'I'd much rather stay here looking after you and Mercia and Richard,' she protested, unable to meet Tamily's eyes.

Jess, watching the girl's flushed cheeks, said gently:

'Tamily and I can manage quite easily here, Sandra. Adam has nobody and you know how busy he is with the harvesting.'

So Sandra went down to Adam's house to cook and clean for him. She tried to arrange her hours there so that she would be sure not to see him. For two days she succeeded and then he came home unexpectedly with a badly gashed finger he had caught in one of the balers. He looked pleased and a little embarrassed finding her there but the first moment of shyness wore off when she saw his hand. Calmly and expertly she held it under the tap, examined the wound and dressed it, telling him he was lucky he didn't need any stitches.

Adam smiled.

'I forgot you wanted to be a nurse. You're a very good one, too. Why didn't you go on with your career?' he asked.

Colour flooded the girl's cheeks and she turned away, dropping his hand quickly.

'Perhaps I'm just not a career girl,' she said lightly.

211

'No, maybe not!' Adam agreed. 'A girl like you would expect to get married–' He broke off, realising he was now on dangerous ground. Suddenly, he didn't care. He'd wanted so much to see her, talk to her, try to make her realise he needed her. Now was his chance and even if she hated him for it, he wasn't going to miss the opportunity.

'Sandra!' he said quietly. 'I know you've been avoiding me. It's worried me very much. Do you hate me – for what happened?'

She felt her heart thudding so furiously she was afraid he might hear it. He sounded humble, no, hurt was a better description.

'No, no, of course not!' She turned then and looked at him. 'I'm sorry if you thought that. I thought you knew how I felt. None of it was *your* fault. I made you. I wanted it to happen. I'm not sorry.'

His face cleared. He almost smiled.

'I'm so glad. I'm not sorry either – or ashamed. I know I ought to be – I ought not to have taken advantage of you the way I did, but … well, I just couldn't help myself. I'm glad you don't hate me.'

'Oh, Adam!' Suddenly there were tears in her eyes. Was it really possible he could be so blind to the truth? Didn't he realise that pride forbade her from becoming a burden to him? His offer to marry her had been, in a way, a humiliation. It was so like Adam to feel he had to do the honourable thing. No wonder she had avoided him. She'd thought he would forget all about that night and everything could continue as it always had. But it did not work out that way. Adam seldom came to Lower Beeches any more. He no longer saw much of Tamily and Sandra had wondered if he was avoiding the house because she, Sandra, was there.

'Look, Sandra!' Adam was on his feet, his bandaged hand outstretched towards her in unconscious appeal. 'I know you don't want to talk about it – I can understand you wishing it had never happened and I wouldn't blame you for hating me. But we can't go on as if it hadn't happened – or at least, I can't. Somehow it changed everything in my life. Nothing has been the same since. I suppose you made me realise how much I was missing. I've never had much to do with women and maybe something like that had to happen to me to make me see that I can't go on living alone. I need you, Sandra. Not just any woman. I need you. Is the idea of marriage to me so distasteful? I'd do everything in my power to make you happy.'

Sandra heard him out in silence. This was a new, different Adam. There was no talk now of it being his duty to marry her. He said he needed her. If she could only believe that.

'I'd marry you, Adam,' she said softly,

looking directly into his eyes, 'if you could tell me that you aren't still in love with Tamily.'

Adam drew in his breath sharply.

'I won't lie to you, Sandra – not to you. The truth is, I just don't know the answer to that question. I've always believed I was in love with her. I think in a way I always shall love her. But everything has changed. It changed the night you and I were together. I left Tamily, wanting her desperately, as a man does want the woman he loves. Then you appeared out of the darkness and I accepted what I suppose was a substitute for my need of Tamily. But then, suddenly, it wasn't like that. It was you, Sandra, I held in my arms; you I wanted; to you that I made love. Tamily had no part in it and hasn't in my dreams which have been only of you. I can't explain any better than that, Sandra. I just don't understand it myself. If I really love Tamily as I believed, how could I replace her so easily and so permanently with you? I want to say to you: I love you. I love and need you desperately. But I'm afraid to use the word love for I am no longer sure of its meaning. All I am sure of is my need of you.'

She was looking at him now, her eyes large and shining and filled with shy delight. She didn't care if he couldn't say he loved her. It was enough that he needed her. She didn't really mind him saying he would always love Tamily – so would she. It was impossible not to love her but at least Adam wasn't in love with her. If he were, he'd be sure.

Adam was looking at her, his eyes anxious, searching her face. She said softly:

'I don't know how to answer you. I love you, Adam. I've always loved you – since I was still at school. But I know I couldn't share you – I'm really a horrible character– I'm jealous and I hate myself for it. I know what Tamily has meant to you.'

'And I don't deny it – but that phase of my life has come to an end, Sandra. If you want, I'll give up my job. We'll buy a farm some-where and go right away from the Allentons – make a fresh start, together.'

Sandra stared at him disbelievingly.

'You really mean that, Adam? You'd give up your life here – for me?'

Adam nodded. He had not been sure of it until he spoke but now he knew it was true. He loved this place, had always looked on it as his home and the Allentons as if they were his own family but now he knew that he was prepared to leave everything if Sandra asked him; if it meant he would have a real home of his own, a wife and family of his own.

'Then I will marry you!' Sandra's voice was firm and filled with joy. 'And I don't want you to leave the Allentons. It's enough to know that you would have done so for me. We'll stay here – together.'

A moment later Adam's arms were around her, holding her to him. He was unprepared for the rush of love he felt for her. He thought humbly that he didn't deserve such a girl. She really loved him and as if she had not already proved it that night in the woods, then she had proved it now by her offer to stay here and marry him, despite the fact that he would be bound to see Tamily at times.

'Maybe we should go away – start afresh somewhere,' he murmured against her hair. But she shook her head.

'No, Adam, I'm not running away. I was afraid before but I'm not now. It would break Lord Allenton's heart if you went – he relies on you completely, especially with Dick away. And I know you love this place. I do, too. It's as much a part of my life as it is yours. I can be happy here – with you!' she added shyly.

'Oh, my darling!' Adam said huskily. Then he bent his head and very tenderly he kissed her. He felt her arms, warm and soft, tighten around his neck. Everything about her seemed warm and inviting, strong yet yielding in his embrace.

'Sandra, Sandra!' he whispered. 'Let's not wait too long to be married. I don't want to go on living here without you now. How strange it is! I've been content here alone – or thought I was. Now I realise suddenly how desperately empty my life has been.'

'And mine!' Sandra whispered back. 'I love you so much, Adam.'

'And I love you!' The words were torn from him and as they formed on his lips, he knew quite suddenly that it was true. He did love her ... and he knew with a strange certainty that it was a love which would grow with time. He was filled with a breathless tenderness for the girl in his arms. Nothing should ever hurt her. He would cherish her, keep her eyes full of stars as they were now. He wanted to shout with joy – to rush off and tell everyone of the miracle that had happened. And yet he never, never wanted to let go of her.

'When?' he asked breathlessly, feeling as if the years had slipped away from him and he was a boy again, filled with impatience and longing. 'When will you marry me, my Sandra?'

'Soon!' She was so happy she wanted to cry. It was nearly impossible to believe that this was Adam; that he really did love her, want her; that she was going to live here – in this house, with him, his wife. Yes, she would marry him soon for indeed she had waited quite long enough; they had wasted enough years. She wanted children while she was still young – children... When Adam had a

217

son of his own, little Richard wouldn't mean so much to him, she thought. He'd no longer even want to spend so much time at Lower Beeches. She could understand now that loneliness had taken him there so often in the past. With a wife and children of his own...

But Adam was kissing her again and she stopped thinking of anything in the world except that her cup of happiness was really full at last.

SIXTEEN

The summer was over. In the parks, the leaves were being brushed into heaps and burnt in bonfires which added their grey smoke to the misty atmosphere. Dick walked home to the flat feeling a deep depression of the spirits.

Somehow autumn in the country was quite different from autumn in London. At home, there was a feeling of relaxation after the hard work of the summer harvesting; a feeling of work well done and a quiet peacefulness settling over the fields and woods and lanes as the tempo of life slowed down before the winter. There, the misty mornings and evenings were like a soft kiss without sadness. There, nothing was ending – it was still vibrant and alive beneath the falling leaves as Nature prepared herself for the cold months to come. Squirrels would be hard at work storing their larders; the summer birds had migrated and the winter hardies would be making the most of the shorter daylight hours. On the estate, men would be cutting and sawing wood for the big log fires which would warm them in the way electric fires never could; warming the heart as well as the body.

Dick thought of his horse, restless and anxious to be out, excited by the cold nip in the air. How he'd love a ride! No doubt someone had exercised him – Adam or one of the grooms. But he was Dick's horse and he longed to be up on his back.

Dick's mouth tightened. He wasn't going back home, cap in hand, letting Tamily know he was missing them all desperately. He'd got along these last four months on his own, he told himself as he entered the flat. He was busy at the office in the day and he'd seldom lacked someone to have dinner with at night. For a while, he'd savoured his new-found freedom; his bachelorhood. He'd seen most of the good shows; had one or two drinking parties. And then, of course, there was Muriel…

Dick's face clouded. In a way, he felt guilty about Muriel. She'd proved a damn good friend and he wished she hadn't had to get hurt in the process. Once or twice he'd nearly weakened and become her lover. Maybe if he hadn't known she was in love with him, he might have drifted into the affair he knew she wanted. But she was serious about him and he hadn't wanted to become involved, knowing very well that he didn't love her.

Dick poured himself a drink and sat down in the empty sitting-room, his face brooding.

'I've changed!' he thought with surprise. There was a time when he'd never have given a thought to the moral issue. It wasn't even as if he felt he owed it to Tam to stay faithful to her. She'd walked out on him and all but told him to go to Muriel. She thought they were having an affair and he would have been quite justified, he told himself, in letting himself be the black sheep she thought him. But somehow, attractive as Muriel was, he'd avoided letting their friendship develop beyond the mildest flirtation.

Deep down, he'd known Muriel wanted more from him. Fortunately, they'd both been frantically busy getting the Club started and once it was open, he'd had his hands full every weekend coping with the water ski-ing venture. And a howling success it had been, too. At least he'd been able to give Muriel that in return for her friendship and generosity. As Muriel herself had said when they closed the lake down for the winter, he'd more than earned his share of the profits when the day of reckoning came. His idea had put the Club on its feet – made it one of the most popular places for the smart young set to go. They were fully booked all through the summer and neither he nor Muriel doubted that they'd be back next summer. Many of their clients were booking already for Muriel's Christmas

Gala Week.

Dick frowned. He wished there were some way he could let Tamily know just how wrong she'd been to scorn his plans. She'd had no faith in him and he'd proved her wrong. Muriel had already been approached by an American who wanted to buy the Club. But she wasn't selling yet – despite the high price he offered. Dick thought it a fair price but Muriel told him coolly that by next summer, he'd be willing to pay half as much again. Dick didn't argue – she obviously knew what she was about and he was more than content to know that he would have recouped all his losses at the very least. Moreover, Muriel had been decent enough to offer to buy back his shares whenever he wanted.

He thought of her now with real affection. Somehow, she'd guessed his restlessness as the season came to a close. She'd known the continual weekends down at the Club had lost their novelty and that the fun had gone out of it for him.

'You'd like to be at home, wouldn't you, Dick? Farming!'

Dick had tried to laugh it off. But Muriel persisted.

'We're partners, Dick, and I know I owe you a lot. It was your idea which really made the Club successful from the word go. You've put an enormous amount of work in here, too, and so far, you've had nothing out of it. I want you to know I'm willing to buy your shares back – at a fair price. You can have your capital now.'

'Trying to get rid of me?' Dick said lightly, uneasy because she had somehow given his sub-conscious longings a name and he didn't want to think about Lower Beeches, about Tam, the farm. He couldn't go back...

He was unprepared for Muriel's reply.

'You must know I don't want to be rid of you, Dick. I've been crazy about you from the night we met. No, don't interrupt. I know damn well you don't feel the same way about me. Why should you? You're years younger than I am and anyway, you're still in love with that wife of yours. I suppose I was a fool ever to start hoping you might stop loving the girl. When you told me you'd agreed to separate, I warned myself not to start getting ideas. But ... well, we can't always control our emotions, worst luck, and next thing, I was hoping you might one day think of taking our "business partnership" a stage further. I knew you weren't in love with me but I hoped you might find me attractive enough to want me – for a little while anyway. But your heart's not in it, is it, Dick? You and your energies and ideas have been here but your heart is still down at that country seat of yours!'

Yes, Muriel was a decent sort. He'd hated

hurting her but sensibly, she'd handled what could have been a very embarrassing situation in such a way that they'd parted the best of friends.

'Perhaps I was a fool!' Dick told himself, pouring out another drink. 'Perhaps I should have taken what she offered me. One thing's sure and that is my own wife doesn't love me!'

There had been not one word from Tamily. No letter, no phone call – nothing at all to indicate that she was regretting their separation or that she'd changed her mind about anything. The only news he had of the children were brief letters from his father and mother, telling him that the children were well and giving him news of the farm. They never mentioned Tamily.

In their last letter, they'd informed him that Adam and Sandra were getting married. The news had shaken him quite a bit. Somehow he'd gone on thinking of Adam dancing attendance on Tamily in his absence – being a proxy father to the children – perhaps even a proxy husband, too!

'We all hope you'll come down for the wedding,' his mother had written. 'It will be on October 12th.'

Dick was reminded painfully of other weddings at their lovely village church. His sister, Mercia's. She'd looked so lovely, so radiantly happy. And then his own, to

Tammy. No bride could have been more beautiful – at least, not in his eyes. How happy everyone had been that day – not a soul in the village who could walk had failed to turn out to wish them joy. And how desperately in love they'd been…

Dick's face tightened with sudden emotion. How was it possible for marriages to go so wrong? Whose fault was it? His? Tammy's? Both, perhaps. But he'd tried. Maybe at first it was his fault – he'd been self-centred and finally unfaithful and he'd nearly lost Tam for good and all. But since then, he'd done everything he possibly could to make it up to her. He'd really loved her more than he'd believed possible. So why had it all gone wrong again? Tamily said she'd forgiven him but deep down she hadn't. She'd jumped to the conclusion he was up to something with Muriel when she should have trusted him, believed in him. How could a man believe in himself when his wife had no faith in him?

But he knew that wasn't really the cause of their separation. It was the boy – the boy's deafness. Tamily couldn't seem to under-stand why the sight of the child upset him; made him almost physically sick to see him. It was probably worse for him because he knew that he was responsible – almost certainly responsible. In a way, he could understand Tam hating him because of the way he felt about the boy. She was the child's mother and, no doubt about it, she would certainly have a strong protective maternal instinct. If only he could feel differently.

He realised that it was months now since he'd seen Richard. Had he grown a lot? Had he changed? Kids of that age did change so quickly when they were small. Maybe he wouldn't even know his own son if he saw him...

Suddenly Dick had an urgent desire to see him. He wouldn't stay, of course – just go down for a quick visit. He could find some excuse – finances, the farm, something, to take him down tomorrow afternoon. Little Mercia would give him a welcome if no one else did.

Saturday morning broke fine and sunny. An Indian summer's day with only a hint of chill behind the warmth of the sun. With London behind him, Dick really began to enjoy the drive. The countryside looked neat and tidy – hedges, cut, ploughing already started, haystacks covered with tarpaulins. Some of yesterday's depression left him. Tomorrow wasn't so important. Today he was going to enjoy himself. He was going home.

At the Lodge House there was no sign of Adam but Dick noticed the garden had been newly dug and that some of the heavy laurel bushes which had overgrown near the house had been dug up and removed. There were new curtains hanging in the front windows. Dick smiled. Another ten days and Adam would be taking Sandra to the altar – how silly he'd been to imagine that Adam and Tamily...

He turned off the main drive on to the lane which led to Lower Beeches. As he approached the old red-brick farmhouse, he slowed down the car and caught his breath. Nowhere – no house in the world, was quite like this, soft, mellowed, part of the gentle lawns and sweeping beech trees that surrounded it. How lovingly this house had been built all those centuries ago – to blend and merge with the beauty around it.

He pulled the car up by the front door but the house seemed deserted. He stood looking at the oak door for a moment or two and then turned away and walked across the lawn round to the south side. A few late roses were still blooming in the flowerbeds. The beech leaves were fluttering slowly on to the cut grass.

Suddenly a small child came running towards him, fat sturdy legs still unsure of themselves. Dick caught his breath. This, surely, wasn't Richard – the boy was too old. Yet he knew that it was. His heart missed a beat.

Two solemn blue eyes stared up at him from beneath a thatch of fair, curly hair. And round the children's neck, across the red jersey, lay the thin wire of the boy's deaf aid. Dick caught his lip. If only … if only…

A star-fish hand pointed up at him. The soft red lips parted and the boy said:

'Man? Man?'

For a moment, Dick couldn't reply. It was the first word he had ever heard Richard speak. Suddenly, he dropped on one knee and looking into the boy's face, he shook his head.

'Not Man – Dad, Dad!' he said.

The boy's face broke into a smile, trusting, friendly.

'Man!' he said again. Then he touched Dick's face. 'Nose!' He laughed again and changed feet in a curious little jump. He took Dick's hand and pulled at it.

'Bike!' he said. He pointed towards a small tricycle overturned on the grass. 'Bike, Bike!' he repeated, pulling harder at Dick's hand. Dick got up and, hand in hand with his son, walked over to the tricycle, stood it upright and watched Richard scramble on to the seat. A moment later, the boy was pedalling away from him at what seemed to Dick to be a very dangerous speed. The tricycle wobbled alarmingly as the boy swung round in a sharp circle and came back towards him.

'Watch out!' Dick called instinctively and then broke off grinning. What was the fun of going slowly! A boy was a boy – he wanted speed, not safety. Dick thought, 'He isn't just a boy any more – he's Jim Clark – an engine driver...'

As he watched, Sandra came out from the French windows and nodded at Richard. The boy pedalled furiously towards her.

'He'd better slow up!' the thought crossed Dick's mind. 'He'll crash into her!' But at that second, Richard swerved into a hairpin bend, the bike wobbled and then he found his balance and shot off again round the lawn, ending up beside Dick.

Dick was grinning.

'Why, you little devil!' he said. 'You did that on purpose – just to frighten poor Sandra!'

The child was flushed, smiling.

'Sanda! Sanda!' he said, looking at Dick speculatively, knowing he'd been naughty. But the man did not look cross. He looked even pleased. Richard pressed home his advantage.

'Go! Me ... go!'

'All right, off you go!' Dick said. But the boy frowned. He pushed the tricycle away and pointed down across the lawns to the paddock. A Shetland pony was grazing, its broad rump turned towards them.

'Go!' Richard said again, once more tugging at Dick's hand.

'Well, I don't know!' Dick said hesitantly. Was it Richard's pony? Surely a child of his age – a handicapped child at that – wasn't allowed to ride yet. On the other hand, whose pony was it? It was too small for Mercia. Where was Tamily? Ought he to let the boy near the pony?

Sandra came across the lawn towards them.

'What a nice surprise!' she said. 'I thought it was you but I wasn't quite sure.'

'Look, Sandra, Richard seems to want to go on the pony. Is he allowed?'

Sandra laughed.

'He's allowed, so long as someone is with him. He's a little terror – if you turn your back for two seconds, he's trying to make poor little Shandy gallop. Never a moment's peace with this one!' She tousled Richard's already untidy hair. 'Do you know, he was up the apple tree yesterday – and down it. Before we got him, he was trying to get up again. You just can't leave him for a moment. And we used to think Mercia was a bother at this age!'

Richard was tired of waiting. His small body, square and determined, was already halfway across the lawn. Watching him, Dick felt a strange lump in his chest – a swelling of emotion that he could not explain was pride.

'I was just as bad according to Mother!' he said as he and Sandra walked slowly after the boy. 'Broke the greenhouse windows when I was three. How he's grown, Sandra! I can't believe it.'

'I know. And he's made such wonderful progress with his talking.' Sandra's voice was quite natural. If Dick was uneasy by her reference to Richard's deaf aid, she was unaware of it. 'He can say twenty words perfectly clearly, and he knows what they mean, too. Sometimes he can't get the whole word out – he calls Adam, Dam, which always makes us laugh.'

'That reminds me, I have to congratulate you both.'

Sandra looked happy and said:

'You will be down for the wedding, won't you? It just wouldn't be the same if you weren't there.'

Dick did not reply. He didn't want to think about tomorrow and the next day. He didn't want to think about the wretched failure of his marriage to Tamily. For a moment he hated Sandra for bringing him face to face again with his problems. He'd been so happy enjoying his little son.

Sandra opened the paddock gate and Dick stood watching as she lifted the little boy on to the pony's back. It was a very fat pony and immensely docile. The child was obviously perfectly safe on its back. He clutched at its mane and dug his sandals into the pony's bulging sides. Sandra laughed and started to walk forward. The pony followed her.

Richard's face was a mask of impatience. It was clear to Dick that he wanted to go faster – faster. He grinned. Just like himself at that age – a real boy.

'Well, Dick?'

He'd been so absorbed in Richard he hadn't heard Tamily come up behind him; had not realised she stood there studying not the child's face but his own as he proudly regarded his son.

Dick cleared his throat. He was suddenly unable to speak. Tamily was wearing faded blue denim jeans and a white sleeveless polo-necked shirt. It accentuated her golden-brown sunburnt arms, neck and face. She looked very fit – the lines of tension quite gone from her face; younger and more relaxed, though thin.

'But you always were thin!' he spoke aloud.

'You've lost weight, too!' Tamily said softly. She was a little shocked by his appearance. He looked tired, lined – so much older.

'Well, there's someone in the family who puts on weight!' he nodded at Richard. 'I hardly recognised him. I should congratulate you, Tam. He's a fine little boy now.'

'And tough as old leather–' Tamily began eagerly, then broke off. Tough or not, Richard was still in Dick's eyes handicapped. It must have been pity, not pride, she'd seen in his face as she came quietly up to him.

Silence lay between them, a silence that neither could seem to overcome. There was so much Tamily wanted to know – why was he here? Why today? How long had he come for? But pride forbade her questioning him. And he too, had so much he wanted to ask. Had she missed him? Was she happy without him? What of the future?

Suddenly unable to bear the awkwardness, Tamily said:

'How's the Country Club?'

Glad to have the silence broken, Dick said quickly:

'Oh, fine! The season is over, of course, and I won't be going down there any more. It's been a fabulous success. I'll make a lot of money out of it–' he broke off. Tamily said:

'I'm glad – for you, I mean. I've been proved wrong, haven't I? I took it for granted it would fail.'

Her words disarmed him. He said:

'Oh, well, most of my gambles have failed in the past. Small wonder you doubted the wisdom of this one. I've just been lucky – and Muriel's a wonderful business woman. It was mostly due to her.'

Tamily looked down at her hands, biting her lip.

She could guess now why Dick was here. He'd made money at last and now he could afford to have the divorce he no doubt wanted. He wanted to marry the woman who had believed in him, encouraged him. He'd come to ask her for his freedom.

'I won't stand in your way!' The words were torn from her.

Dick looked at her frowning.

'Stand in my way? What do you mean, Tamily?'

'If you ... if you want a divorce!'

'A divorce?' Dick repeated stupidly. 'But why? You don't think—' he broke off, suddenly laughing. 'You don't really think I want to marry Muriel? Why, she's years older than I am and, anyway, I'm not in the least in love with her.'

Tamily caught her breath. The relief was so intense she couldn't think of anything else. For months now she'd imagined Dick and Muriel having a marvellous time together, in love, sharing all the wonderful moments which she'd once shared with Dick. She'd been eaten up with jealousy and despair because she'd been slowly forced to realise that their separation wasn't Dick's fault this time, but hers. The teacher who came to help Richard had now become one of her best friends. Through her Tamily had been made to realise that Dick's reactions to Richard's handicap were understandable, instinctive reactions which were echoed by other parents. All he'd needed was a little time, a lot of tact, and there need have been no argument about Richard at all. Dick had always loved the baby and he'd have gone on loving him – most parents did when the initial shock wore off. Jess, too, had forced her to face up to the fact that for Dick, it was so much harder than for her.

'You know how he always loathed illness!' Jess reminded her. 'Perhaps you were too young at the time to realise but it was torture for him when Mercia was in that wheel-chair. He was always so healthy himself, too. It isn't that Dick is insensitive, Tamily – it's that he's over-sensitive. His horror isn't just his own but for Richard, too.'

At first Tamily hadn't wanted to believe it. It was much easier to hate Dick – to feel bitter and resentful towards him; to be convinced that the breakdown in their marriage was all his fault. But as the weeks passed and there was no word from him, as Richard grew and began slowly to talk and her loneliness and longing for him grew, she began to face up to the truth. Seeing Adam and Sandra so much in love, so happy together, so often hand in hand, unwilling to be far away from each other for long, she'd come to realise that in the end a woman could not devote her whole life to her children. She needed the love and companionship of a man, too, and the only man in the world for her was Dick.

'Why did you come then?' The words were

wrung from her like a cry of pain.

'Why?' Dick sighed. 'I suppose because I just had to see you. I told myself it was Richard I wanted to see, I thought he might quite easily have forgotten me – he has, too – do you know, he called me, "Man"!' His smile was not a happy one. 'But what's the point in kidding oneself – I wanted to see you, Tam. It's been such ages. I–'

He broke off, staring at her, miserable and desperate, longing to sweep her into his arms and yet not able to touch her.

'I suppose, as always, I've been a bloody fool.'

'Oh, Dick, no. I'm the one who's been silly. It was all my fault. I couldn't bear it because you seemed to turn against Richard. It ... it seemed so unfair and he needed both of us so much. I ought to have seen that it wasn't Richard you were hating but Fate which had made him deaf.'

'Hate him?' Dick almost shouted. 'Don't you see it was because I loved him so much I felt there just had to be something better for him than ... than a deaf aid. But I was wrong about it, not you. Why, do you know he can say twenty words – different words – and I could understand him, too. "Go, bike, man" – they were perfectly clear and Sandra says...' He broke off grinning. 'But of course you know ... you were the one who taught him.'

There were tears in Tamily's eyes although she was smiling.

'Dick, you sound so proud of him!'

'And so I am. Why shouldn't I be? He's a wonderful kid, Tamily, and not a bit shy. But you've got to teach him to call me "Daddy" and not "Man". That's the next word he's going to learn.'

'Dick, wouldn't you … couldn't you … what I'm trying to say is, must it be me? Must I teach him? Or would you?'

He looked into her eyes, read what lay behind her words and knew she was asking him to stay with them. As if he needed *asking*.

'Yes, I'll teach him!' he said. 'And I'll teach him to ride properly, too. That pony's far too fat for him. Look at his legs! And he needs something with a bit of "go" in it. That boy's got guts, Tamily. Walking round the field isn't going to satisfy him for long.'

Tamily smiled tremulously.

'Oh, Dick, he's not yet three!'

Dick put his arms round her and held her tightly. He was so happy he wanted to shout.

'If he's this spunky at two, he's certainly going to need some paternal discipline,' he said. 'Can't have you turning my son into a mother's boy.'

Tamily nestled her head against Dick's chest and chuckled.

'That's not very likely, Dick. He's far too much like you!'

The boy was off the pony now, running towards them, ahead of Sandra. He stood in front of them, legs apart and looked up at Dick.

'Man? Man?' he said.

'No, Dad!' said Dick. He let Tamily go and knelt down beside the boy, his arm round the child's shoulders, his face suddenly gentle but determined. 'Try it, old chap – say, "Dad, Dad". It isn't difficult.'

'Dad, Dad?' said Richard.

'That's my boy!' said Dick. He scooped him up into his arms and, across the fair curly head, his eyes met Tamily's shining at him with pride and love.